# FRESH FIRE

*from the "Triumphant Living" series*

# FRESH FIRE

*Spiritual Transitions That Lead to Total Man Rebirth*

## by Mark L. Spell

"And from the days of John the Baptist until now the kingdom of heaven suffereth violence, and the violent take it by force."
-Matthew 11:12

ReadersMagnet, LLC

*Fresh Fire: Spiritual Transitions That Lead To Total Man Rebirth*
Copyright © 2020 by Mark L. Spell

Published in the United States of America
ISBN Paperback: 978-1-953616-36-4
ISBN eBook: 978-1-953616-37-1

This book is written to provide information and motivation to readers. Its purpose is not to render any type of psychological, legal, or professional advice of any kind. The content is the sole opinion and expression of the author, and not necessarily that of the publisher.

All rights reserved. No part of this publication may be reproduced, stored in a retrieval system or transmitted in any way by any means, electronic, mechanical, photocopy, recording or otherwise without the prior permission of the author except as provided by USA copyright law.

ReadersMagnet, LLC
10620 Treena Street, Suite 230 | San Diego, California, 92131 USA
1.619.354.2643 | www.readersmagnet.com

Book design copyright © 2020 by ReadersMagnet, LLC. All rights reserved.
*Cover design by Ericka Obando*
*Interior design by Shemaryl Tampus*

# Contents

Preface . . . . . . . . . . . . . . . . . . . . . . . . . . . . . . . . . . . . . . . . . .1
Endure For The Joy . . . . . . . . . . . . . . . . . . . . . . . . . . . . . . .3
Introduction . . . . . . . . . . . . . . . . . . . . . . . . . . . . . . . . . . . .5
Why the Tombs? . . . . . . . . . . . . . . . . . . . . . . . . . . . . . . . .7
Triumphant Living (Dare to Do!) . . . . . . . . . . . . . . . . . .25
The Power to Overcome Catastrophe . . . . . . . . . . . . . . .43
Blessed, Anointed, and Highly Favored . . . . . . . . . . . . .57
The Next Best Thing . . . . . . . . . . . . . . . . . . . . . . . . . . .71
Fight The Devil On His Terms . . . . . . . . . . . . . . . . . . . .89
Hope . . . . . . . . . . . . . . . . . . . . . . . . . . . . . . . . . . . . . . .109
The Improbable Move Of God . . . . . . . . . . . . . . . . . . .123
Inside Out . . . . . . . . . . . . . . . . . . . . . . . . . . . . . . . . . . .137
Reader Testimonies . . . . . . . . . . . . . . . . . . . . . . . . . . . .153

Why The Tombs? . . . . . . . . . . . . . . . . . . . . . . . . . . . . .157
Triumphant Living: Dare To Do! . . . . . . . . . . . . . . . . .159
The Power To Overcome Catastrophe . . . . . . . . . . . . .161
The Next Best Thing . . . . . . . . . . . . . . . . . . . . . . . . . .163
Blessed, Anointed, And Highly Favored . . . . . . . . . . . .165
Fight The Devil On His Own Terms . . . . . . . . . . . . . .167

Hope . . . . . . . . . . . . . . . . . . . . . . . . . . . . . . . . . . . . . . . . . 169
The Improbable Move Of God . . . . . . . . . . . . . . . . . . . . . . 171
Inside Out . . . . . . . . . . . . . . . . . . . . . . . . . . . . . . . . . . . 173
About The Author . . . . . . . . . . . . . . . . . . . . . . . . . . . . . 175

# Preface

To God be the glory! Words cannot express how absolutely blessed I am to *finally* have words in print that articulate the awesomeness of the revelations of God in me. Just as he did from the onset of my ministry, the Holy Spirit prompted me to write a book some time ago; however, since then and now, the grace and seasoning of God have abounded such that life experiences have mingled with the knowledge of God in me and have afforded me to walk in a place of wisdom that I did not possess at inception. It is incredible to know that not only has the good prepared me for this work, but the GOOD, BAD, and the UGLY have all worked together to declare me worthy to expound on the principles of triumphant living discussed in this work.

The cover name "Fresh Fire" is a reference to what I believe is the next place that the Lord is taking his people in a world of evolving change and misplaced relevancy. It is fitting that our God would breathe a breath of fresh air on the world and to his people abroad by way of his Word. By the Word of God, we realize the "keys of life." Positive proof that we need the Word now as never before is found in Hosea 4:6, "My People are destroyed for lack of knowledge because thou hast rejected knowledge, I will also reject thee, that thou shalt be no priest to me: seeing thou hast forgotten the law of thy God."

Certainly, in the Word of God, we find a hiding place. The first book in this series is The Keys to Triumphant Living: Vol. 1. In this work, I thought it not robbery to remind the body of

Christ that our Lord and Savior Jesus Christ came, lived, taught, and died that we might have life and that we might have it more abundantly. Knowledge is the principal thing, and the knowledge of the will of God initiates the process of mental, physical, and spiritual deliverance in the life of the believer. So without much ado, I release you to the pages of this book, and I pray that God blesses, strengthens, and enlightens the reader to the point that their very life is forever changed. Amen

"He that receiveth a prophet in the name of a prophet shall receive a prophet's reward; and he that receiveth a righteous man in the name of a righteous man shall receive a righteous man's reward" (Matthew 10:41).

# Endure For The Joy

BY PASTOR MARGARET SPELL

The trials of life are many,
And life's troubles also the same;
But there is joy unspeakable,
Just hold on in Jesus's name.

There are goals to be reached,
More for Christ than for fame;
And th`e God-given favor of victory,
Is much sweeter than earthly gain.
So as Mark Spell goes forward in Jesus,
With childlike faith as a boy;
He will be more than a conqueror,
And have strength to endure
For The Joy

# Introduction

## BY PASTOR MARGARET SPELL

In a time when honesty, honor, decency, integrity, and love seem to become more unappreciated, there remain splashes of manifestations of these virtues still present in men who dare not stray from God's guidance and council.

So has it been with this man of faith, who, as a youth, allowed his will to become lost in the will of kingdom building. Even through loss, hurt, and pain, he continues to overcome the bonds of doubt with faith. Steadfast, focused with the intent to destroy the walls of sinful living by declaring and proclaiming Jesus Christ through living life and teaching in a dark and confused world, he moves forward with commitment.

Through his obedience of our Heavenly Father, prophecy, preaching, healing, and deliverance have touched the lives of hundreds of people near and far. The writing of this book will bless all who seek a daily continuance of faith, joy, and peace.

I am grateful to God for Mark L. Spell, to have known him before anyone else on earth, to have been his first teacher. He was the child that was always giving a helping hand to Momma and Daddy, the one who sought the welfare of his sisters and brother. He is humble and anointed in these last days. Truly, he is appointed in these perilous times to reach the heart of people through the pages of a God-given book that's centered on the Holy Bible.

# Why the Tombs?

A lot of people do not believe that the weapons of our warfare are not carnal. They don't believe that we are not wrestling against flesh and blood. A lot of people refuse the knowledge that what is going on around you is bigger than you. These lessons are an attempt to help us understand the nature of the fight and exactly what we are dealing with and what we need to do to be in a position to be victorious. What we need to do to be in the position to be victorious—THAT'S THE THING THAT WE, AS THE BODY OF CHRIST, MUST CONSIDER. We bless God, his Son, Jesus Christ, and the gift of his Spirit for it takes the Holy Spirit to take us beyond that that we have not seen before. Christians do not have to be victims. The enemy is all about victimizing the body of Christ, and it is important to know that being a victim is not a prerequisite for being in the body.

> And they came over unto the other side of the sea, into the country of the Gadarenes. And when he was come out of the ship, immediately there met him out of the tombs a man with an unclean spirit, who had his dwelling among the tombs; and no man could bind him, no not with chains: Because that he had been often bound with fetters and chains, and the chains had been plucked asunder by him, and the fetters broken in pieces: neither could any man tame him. And always, night and day, he was in the mountains, and in the tombs,

crying, and cutting himself with stones. But when he saw Jesus afar off, he ran and worshipped him, and cried with a loud voice, and said, "What have I to do with thee, Jesus, thou Son of the Most High God? I adjure thee by God, that thou torment me not." For he said unto him, "Come out of the man, thou unclean spirit." And he asked him, "What is thy name?" And he answered, saying, "My name is Legion: for we are many." And he besought him much that he would not send them away out of the country. Now there was there nigh unto the mountains a great herd of swine feeding. And all the devils besought him, saying, send us into the swine, that we may enter into them. And forth–with Jesus gave them leave. And the unclean spirits went out, and entered into the swine: and the herd ran violently down a steep place into the sea, (they were about two thousand;) and were choked in the sea. And they that fed the swine fled, and told it in the city, and in the country. And they went out to see what it was that was done. And they come to Jesus, and see him that was possessed with the devil, and had the legion, sitting, and clothed, and in his right mind: and they were afraid. And they that saw it told them how it befell to him that was possessed with the devil, and also concerning the swine. And they began to pray him to depart out of their coasts. And when he was come into the ship, he that had been possessed with the devil prayed him that he might be with him. Howbeit Jesus suffered him not, but saith unto him, go home to thy friends, and tell them how great things the Lord hath done for thee, and hath had compassion on thee. (Mark 5:1–19)

Powerful Word here. This is not an unfamiliar scripture for it is commonly numbered with the most popular themes found in the Word of God. However, what is unfamiliar is the question the Spirit of the Living God is asking in this chapter concerning the text. Why the tombs? To fully wrap your mind around that question, one must understand that there is not much that this man, after having been possessed with demons, does that he is in charge of or has control of. It is important to gather that if this man is in the tombs, it is not by his choosing that he is there, but he is there because of the supernatural influence of the demonic spirits that have possessed his natural body. So once you wrap your mind around the fact that he is in the tombs because of the spirits that have possessed him and taken charge of his body, mind, and will, the question "Why the tombs?" becomes even more involved and intriguing. Even more mind provoking is the understanding that demons are perfectly at home amongst DEAD THINGS.

It is important to note that when the enemy binds a man, one of the ways he goes about binding him is that he works through the annals of familiarity to bind in such a way that we cannot go forward and live out the creed and purpose in Christ that is to be birthed in our future and not our past. He works to tie us to dead things or to things from our past that we have no power over in terms of being able to bring them any closer to anything that resembles victory. So many of us are bound even though we are alive. We are bound by hurt. We are bound by pain. We are bound by rejection. All these things that are familiar, all these things that are dead, all these things that bring us no closer to realizing our purpose, however the spirit that binds are comfortable dealing in these dead things.

It is essential to note that it was impossible to discern in the flesh where the man stopped and Legion started. Only Jesus, through the infinite wisdom of the Father, had the ability to bring about delineation between the man and the spirits operating in the man under the auspices of being the man. Look at the second verse of our text scripture, "And when he was come out of the ship, immediately there met him out of the tombs a man with an unclean spirit."

In this, we find that the unclean spirit would be manifested in the only way the natural man can recognize, and that is through the flesh, and therefore be interpreted as the man misbehaving. Therefore, people who had dealings with the man called the misguiding of Legion as the man. It is important for the true-born believer to understand and entertain that we are not necessarily who and what we want to be or who we would like to think that we are, but we are what we continue to do. CONSISTENCY DEFINES A MAN! Not one's mental projection of your physical self. No wonder Paul declared in Roman 7:14–25,

> For we know that the law is spiritual: but I am carnal, sold under sin. For that which I do I allow not: for what I would, that do I not; but what I hate, that do I. If then I do that which I would not, I consent unto the law that it is good. Now then it is no more I that do it, but sin that dwel-leth in me. For I know that in me (that is, in my flesh,) dwelleth no good thing: for to will is present with me; but how to perform that which is good I find not. For the good that I would I do not: but the evil which I would not, that I do. Now if I do that I would not, it is no more I that do it, but sin that dwelleth in me. I find then a law, that, when I would do good, evil is present with me. For I delight in the law of God after the inward man: But I see another law in my members, warring against the law of my mind, and bringing me into captivity to the law of sin which is in my members. O wretched man that I am! Who shall deliver me from the body of this death? I thank God through

Jesus Christ our Lord. So then with the mind I myself serve the law of God; but with the flesh the law of sin.

So the Bible declares that HE had an unclean spirit. Later, we find out that he had more than just one unclean spirit. It is obvious through the text scripture that most people who dealt with the man knew that he had an unclean spirit; however, it took Jesus and the influence of the anointing of the Holy Spirit to move the man from a place of generalizations to determination, to specification and deliverance. As long as we are led and deceived by the enemy to only believe generally that something is wrong and never move to a place of getting to the root of what is wrong and then exercising the power of the Holy Spirit to take control of the moment to progress to our future-designed purpose in God, we will never TRIUMPH over the times of our lives that serve as the directional markers provided by God to lead us to our designed purpose in him.

So the pronouns utilized in the text bear understanding to differentiate which of the subjects of this text are being referred to. Yes, we have two subjects in this text that are occupying the same space. The man and the demons that have possessed him. Let's take a closer look at the pronouns found in our text.

> Who had his dwelling among the tombs; and no man could bind him, no, not with chains: Because that he had been often bound with fetters and chains, and the chains had been plucked asunder by him, and the fetters broken in pieces: neither could any man tame him. And always, night and day, he was in the mountains, and in the tombs, crying, and cutting himself with stones. (Mark 5:3–5)

Who is being referred to here, his, him, he, him, he, or himself? It is clear now, through the discerning eyes of the Holy Spirit, that the demons are being referred to and not the man. It is the legions that had their dwelling amongst the tombs, and the man is held hostage to their dominance. It is the legions that supernaturally controlled the man's physical ability with an insane display that caused the man's body to respond to human contact absent of thought and rendered the man impossible to bind. And it is legions that caused the man to experience tremendous highs (mountain experiences) and treacherous lows (in the dumps). The man is simply being held hostage (most times) to the spirits that dominate him. So it is clearer now that the man is in the tombs not because that is where he wants to be but because it is where Legion wants to be and where the man has come to realize he can be.

Many are not living the life they want to live, but they are living the life that they can live. When the man was being chased off by men who recognized his uncleanness, he was being chased from where he wanted to be to where he could be and the demons wanted to be all the time. When he was being driven from the synagogue because of the nature of his obvious bondage, he was being chased from where he wanted to be to where the demons were trying to drive him. WHY DO DEMONS WANT TO LIVE IN THE GRAVEYARD?

Familiarity. Even though demons cannot possess dead bodies, they are still directly influenced by the remembrance of what used to be. For you and I, it is important to note that it is very possible for Christians to be bound by what USED to be. It is important to know that when the enemy comes up against us like a flood, he is coming with remembrances of people, places, and things from our past. When he comes to tempt us, it matters little how much we have been shouting, speaking in tongues, or serving in the church. He is not bringing any flavors you have never tasted. He brings the same old stuff we have called home in the past.

He wants you to live in the graveyard. His desire for the believer is that you will live out your lives fighting your past so you will never get to the place where you can live out your future. Your purpose is found in your future. Too many believers are being led into the graveyard simply because, secretly, incognito, under the cover, we are bound by multiple spirits and not just an unclean spirit. That is the reason why you can place Christians with other Christians and somebody will not get along, because someone is living in the graveyard. A lot of the time, we know we have problems. However, what we fail to understand is really how deep the issue runs in us. So the misinterpretation here is we have a SINGLE unclean spirit when actually we have legions. Mark 5:4 says, "Because that he had been often bound with fetters and chains, and the chains had been plucked asunder by him, and the fetters broken in pieces: neither could any man tame him."

It is important to note that when he was not found in the lowest of low, he was to be found in the highest of high. Mood swings can be a sign of demonic activity. When he was not in the valley, he was on the mountaintop. Many church folks don't like it when we speak concerning demons amongst the saints. Saints don't have to be frustrated or upset when the subject comes up simply because the demons we deal with are not necessarily our fault. Legions speak to an army, and an army of demons is not accumulated overnight. Good people…But somebody touched you that should not have touched you and you fell under demonic oppression. People mistreated you, and now your behavior is shaped by past acquaintances—demons. When he was not in the mountains, he was in the graveyard. Have you ever seen people who when they are good, they are excellent, but when they are bad, they are deplorable? "Sometimes up, and sometimes down… almost leveled with the ground." Certainly, this was never God's plan for his people for temperance is one of the fruit of the Spirit as described by Galatians 5:23. Some might ask, "How did this man become susceptible to possession?" I believe a clue to this is found in the fifth verse of our text scripture, "And always, night and day, he was in the mountains, and in the tombs, crying, and cutting himself with stones."

It is important to understand the detriment of self-hatred and a low sense of self-worth and confidence in a child of God. It is a gate for the enemy to come in with demonic activity. There are a lot of people, both of the world and in the church, who simply do not like themselves. So even left alone, he could be found cutting himself. Familiar spirits like familiar bodies and are comfortable in familiar surroundings. We must pray and ask the Lord to help us to not be so afraid of unfamiliar events introduced by the Spirit of God. We must not be afraid to experience new things in God. We must not be afraid to launch out into the deep and try things emotionally in the Lord that you have never tried before. In the process of time, life may have taught you not to trust, but true deliverance for you will be released when you move away from that tomb that says distrust with the incident date of when you were wounded and embrace what is being introduced to you by the Lord as unfamiliar. The enemy wants you to stand right beside that tomb of distrust because that's the body he is familiar with, but the Lord desires to take you to another place, in him, and in order to get you there, he has to pry your hands off your past. Once again, there are a lot of places where we are that we do not necessarily want to be in. Even after we cry salvation or deliverance, there are places in our minds that we find ourselves in from time to time that we do not necessarily want to be. Believe it or not, there are many angry Christians. There are many mad Christians, and the simplest transgression will send them over the deep end. Pinned-up aggression. Many of us simply cannot get where we are going because Satan has us living amongst the tombs. In essence, he is tampering with your victory. He is tampering with your triumphant living. He is inadvertently causing you not to move into those progressions that God has designed for you and working to place you in positions where you cannot live out your true purpose. Back to our text. Look at verse 5, "And always, night and day, he was in the mountains, and in the tombs, crying, and cutting himself with stones."

An excellent question here is, why is he crying? He is crying because he is being tormented. The odd thing is no matter what you do to yourself, as a result of the demons within, they cannot feel the pain. The pain is all yours. Let's make this perfectly clear: no matter what you are doing or what you are involved with as a result of demonic influence, Satan cares absolutely nothing about you. This man is crying because he does not like where he is. He does not like what is going on with him. He does not like that it is him who is living this way. He fully understands that the way he is living is not anyway to live. Even so, he does not have the power to change his world or his reality. There is not one of us who has the power to even change his or her attitude, even less our living conditions. It takes the unadulterated power of GOD to change anything about us. We can point out all day long what needs or could stand to be changed, but if God does not help you change, no change will come. Case in point, we as people can't even change what we admire or are partial to, except when the Spirit of God comes and changes our minds concerning what appeals to us.

So the possessed man is tormented in part because he is being driven to do things that he cannot control. He is being driven by spirits to live in a place where he cannot rebut. Spirits that even the people who he comes in contact with do not understand are driving him. He has already been written off as having an unclean spirit.

Look at verses 6 and 7, "But when he saw Jesus afar off, he ran and worshipped him, and cried with a loud voice, and said, what have I to do with thee, Jesus, thou Son of the Most High God? I adjure thee by God, that thou torment me not."

Who saw Jesus? The man. Not the demon in the man. Catch this: the man, full of demons, worshipped Jesus. He was as full of demons as any person has ever been, yet still he was able to worship Jesus. However, after worshipping, "he" cried with a loud voice. Who cried with a loud voice? The demons. People of God, we must seek the Master's face to have the heart of discernment so that we can discern what is in operation in our midst. It is not always the obvious that is causing the effect. By this example, we understand that at times we grow weary and get frustrated with people when in all actuality it is not the person per se who is speaking. Oftentimes, when people speak, all we are really listening to is hurt, pain, abuse, mistreatment, their LEGION. But without the ear to hear and the wisdom to discern and know that God has an expectation of, we, his people, no matter where we find ourselves, will miss these opportunities in him. It was the man who worshipped but the demons that spoke. Think about those close to you. Oftentimes, we will discount the good because of the bad that follows it. We count the person bad and discount all their good because we give the person credit for the bad and refuse to associate their good with who they are or desire to be. When we fail to understand that there is more in operation than what meets the eye, we remove ourselves from the deliverance equation that God has put forth. Oftentimes, we, the people of God, and even the intercessory, do not understand the nature of the fight. We fall right into the trap. We give up. How many marriages have ended in defeat because of some silent devil that never announced himself? The diagnosis was, "He has an unclean spirit. He is just nasty. He is just filthy. He is just trifling." We attribute all these ungodly attributes to the individual when in all actuality it is not him, but them. As long as we trivialize the supernatural unraveling effect that the devil has on lives, he will continue to wreak havoc on the purpose that God has for our lives. Things are much deeper than they appear. The blessing here is the approach of Jesus. Jesus's approach was one that said, "I am not going to discount you for what came out of your mouth, but I am going to bless you for what you did." Worship reaches God when your deeds do not. If we, the people of God, are going to be spiritual, then we are going to have to be spiritual. We cannot continue to live in both worlds. We must believe that the things we see are driven by the things we cannot see, and by that only are we going to be qualified to wage war in the spirit. We cannot effectively fight in the spirit because we spend too much time in the natural. Half of us are in, and half of us are out. We fail to understand that everything that we see manifested is being driven by what you cannot see. Jesus was armed with this knowledge. Jesus asked, "What is thy name?" Who is going to answer? The demons. "Legion, for we are many." The man is incapacitated. There are people in our lives who in their present state can't altogether help doing what they are doing. There are not bad people; there are bad spirits. It certainly takes the hand of God to give us the wisdom to get to the root of what is really occurring around us. The verse goes on to explain that the demons beckoned unto Jesus not to torment them. It is a peculiar truth that demons will spend an eternity tormenting but not want to be tormented. It is vital that we understand that demons know that their end has already been prescribed; therefore, they seek to wreak as much havoc as they possibly can until they meet their determined end. It is as certain as the rising of the sun that in the judgment, all demons will be thrown in the bottomless pit. All demons. So they make it their business to bring as much destruction to God's creation and to his people as they possibly can. We find in the text scripture that Jesus commands the spirits to come out of the man. We find that the demands became vocal in the scriptures simply because of the command of Jesus that they come out. Jesus recognized the behavior of the man to be that of demons' and not of the man's. At that time, the demons responded, and Jesus asked them who they were. Jesus shed the generalities of "unclean spirit" and stuck to the specifics of "Who are you? What type or kind of demon might you be?" The demon responded with, "We are not demons that govern one specific behavior, but we are legions, armies of demons that govern multitudes of behaviors and mood nomenclatures. We are not just bipolar, but we are psychologically multi-faceted." In offering their given name, we find the cooperative nature of Satan's kingdom. The demons gave their name as their collaborative arrangement dictated. In essence, they described that it was not their name that was important but the nature of their arrangement. "Legion."

If you ever want to know how demons behave or how they approach things, all one has to do is watch people, for it is demons that oftentimes govern how people behave. These particular demons had formulated a pact in the man's body and were actually utilizing it as a sanctuary of sorts, as a gathering place if you will. They had actually "squatted" in this man's body. Demons, army of demons, were a cooperative in the man. They did not talk over each other. They take turns. They practically do the things that we, the people of God, should do as it relates to realizing a common goal in Jesus Christ. They all actively participate in the apparent self-destruction and torment of this man and the inevitable demise of his physical being. The manifestation of their demonic activity was in the flesh. You and I both know that demons are all around; however, they cannot manifest in the earthly realm unless they find a body. Prime example is a demon cannot walk up to you and smack you and you feel it, unless he is in a body. Demons must have a vehicle to interrupt the flow of your natural life. Demons cannot affect man unless he possesses a man, and when he possesses a man, the first thing he does is work to try and cause that man to find his dwelling among the tombs. The most dangerous place for a child of God to reside in is in the annals of their own past. You cannot live in that place called your past. If you want to be taken advantage of by the enemy, live in the past. You will in turn find yourself bitter, angry, hateful, non-trusting—all the things that bind a child of the King and causes him to miss his place and their opportunity to live triumphantly. Why? Because the enemy has separated and caused your existence to be numbered amongst the tombs. The place where demons thrive and long to be. The tombs. Where Satan once ruled your life. The familiar places that he once reigned over in your life. The shadows.

"What is your name?" "Legion, for we are many!"

That question flows from confidence in the power of the Father, which flows from our Lord and Savior. The collective of demons responded with a reply that reflects the impetus to be embolden the enemy has when holding a perceived numbers advantage, with Legion, a threat of sorts if you will. Jesus, of course, is standing in front of a man with a rendering of himself that implies that he is not alone. He indeed implies that he is filled with the spirits of the enemy. Only thing is Jesus is filled with the Spirit of God! The All in All against the all and want to be. Quickly, it becomes evident to the "many" that they are clearly outnumbered! Never forget that your one God is way more than enough for the host of hell! It is never as bad or desperate as Satan is trying to make it out to be. If that devil can cause you to believe that situations are as bad and detrimental as he would like them to appear, "This is something I just cannot deal with," "This is something I just cannot handle," or "This is beyond my ability to even approach," then certainly, he has won. He is always going to swell up and try to embellish the situation and even work to make himself appear more than what he really has the authority to do in a given season.

1 Peter 5:8 says, "Be sober, be vigilant because your adversary the devil, as a roaring lion, walketh about, seeking whom he may devour."

"As a roaring lion" is key here in describing how the enemy represents himself in times of battle; however, it is also implied in the verse that he is not empowered to devour all. The eleventh to thirteenth verses of our text scripture explains,

> Now there was there nigh unto the mountains a great herd of swine feeding. And all the devils

besought him, saying, send us into the swine, that we may enter into them. And forthwith Jesus gave them leave. And the unclean spirits went out, and entered into the swine: and the herd ran violently down a steep place into the sea, (they were about two thousand;) and were choked in the sea. (Mark 5:11–13)

Obviously, this denotes that demons have no desire to be utterly cast out into dark and dry places. They prefer to remain in familiar territories, and to remain, they must have a body. It is also evident in their selection that they knew the purpose of Jesus for men was to heal, deliver, and set free, for they did not request their bodies of preference. Now it is also important to note that the demons needed a quick exit. Pigs are simple beings that lack a soul. That part of us that we obtained when God did in our creating that he did for no other being, and that is he breathed the breath of life and we BECAME a living Soul. Dominance of a man's soul is not an easy undertaking. It is a painstaking process that takes time to master. Demons must pound a man with such a barrage of guilt, self-worthlessness, and low confidence and self-esteem that he willfully, oftentimes unknowingly, relinquishes his God-given right to choose over to him. So even without asking. These demons knew they did not have the time to collectively possess even the weakest mind represented nearby. Even when they possessed the swine, they all separated and went singularly to a pig. Jesus bankrupted the bank of demons that the man had collected over the years and in turn only delayed their return to dark and dry places according to Luke 11:24.

When we fall into a state of depression, you actually lose levels of your spiritual and mental ability to resist the devil. And while you are walking around depressed, it is important to note that demons that are without are seeking ways to get within. And when the ability to war against them is no longer available to you, they will move from the outside of you to the inside of you. And that's why when people are giving in to despair, you see them engaged in levels of craziness like never before. When people give up on life, you find them oftentimes being very promiscuous; you find them given to excessive smoking and drinking and heavy drug usage. They have given up, and demonic forces have taken over. All acts of self-destruction do not necessarily mean the individual wants to do all that they are doing. It simply denotes demonic activity, because they have lost their ability to resist the devil. That's why when you feel the pressure of life is getting to you and you feel yourself slipping into depression, you need to pray and seek to be found around the power and things of God simply because you are under attack and the place the enemy desires to take you is much worse than however you may be feeling at that given time.

> And they that fed the swine fled, and told it in the city, and in the country. And they went out to see what it was that was done. And they come to Jesus, and see him that was possessed with the devil, and had the legion, sitting, and clothed, and in his right mind: and they were afraid. And they that saw it told them how it befell to him that was possessed with the devil, and also concerning the swine. And they began to pray him to depart out of their coasts. And when he was come into the ship, he that had been possessed with the devil prayed him that he might be with him. Howbeit Jesus suffered him not, but saith unto him, Go home to thy friends, and tell them how great things the Lord hath done for thee, and hath had compassion on thee. (Mark 5:14–19)

When these men came and looked on him that was possessed, they were amazed that the man was no longer acting unseemly and crazy. When the spirits and demonic forces were delivered from his mind, a dynamic change was made evident in him. People are behaving the way they are because of demonic possession, and if we can get the spirits out of the people, we will see that people act in ways that would surprise us as it relates to the speed in which deliverance comes.

The man was living in the tombs. He was there. However, we, the learned of God, now understand that he was not in the tombs by choice but as a direct result of demonic possession. We also know that as soon as the demons were cast out of this man, he was prepared to leave the tombs and gravitate to the place where he had self-identified as his purpose in Christ was to be found. The man was prepared to live only after he was delivered from demonic possession. And as soon as he was delivered, he ceased to look behind himself or live in his past and started preparing to live in his present to get to his future. He realized that he now had a future, and that future was in Christ. He had no idea where Jesus was headed, but after deliverance, he knew he wanted to be anywhere Jesus was. Jesus's destination had been there all the time. This man in his past had no purpose in Jesus's destination. Now that he is delivered, he wants to go where he could have gone but had no spiritual connection or purpose to. We understand this because it was not until we were delivered that we had a heart to drive forward and pursue the things of the Most High.

As soon as we get delivered from the rage and the anger and fear that marred our past, we will be able to start the process of "pressing towards the mark of the prize of the high calling in Christ JESUS" (Philippians 3:14). We will start looking towards our purpose as soon as we get delivered from our past. Jesus made it clear to the man that he had a purpose that was not necessarily physically following him. Jesus said, "Go home." Wow! Jesus wanted him to pick up his life and move it backwards to go forward. Newness does not always reflect purpose. Design, intent, anointing, and favor denote purpose. Jesus does not want the picture in him that we present to be in a pause or rewind mode; Jesus wants us in fast-forward.

God did not save us to rage, so we can see better now where we were wronged, but he saved us to lead us to higher ground and to lead us in the path that uncovers our purpose in him. And to get there, we must leave the tombs. There is a place between the tombs and our purpose, the place that transitions us from the graveyard to your purpose, and that place is called Worship. The way out of the graveyard for this man and for us as well is our willingness to worship God wherever we might find ourselves. The man raised those cut-up hands and arms in worship to Jesus and was transformed from being demonically out of his mind to being a minister ordained by Jesus himself.

COME OUT OF THE TOMBS! Come out of the bitterness. Come out of the hurt. Come out of the pain, and allow God to do with you going forward what he will. Triumphant living is yours, but your way to claiming it is found in your worship and your willingness to leave the tombs.

# Triumphant Living (Dare to Do!)

> Then said Jesus unto them again, Verily, verily, I say unto you, I am the door of the sheep. All that ever came before me are thieves and robbers: but the sheep did not hear them. I am the door: by me if any man enters in, he shall be saved, and shall go in and out, and find pasture. (John 10:7–9)

Awesome! Direct contradiction of what most Christians believe in their proper place in God. The scripture prescribes that when you come in through the door called Christ Jesus, things are supposed to get better for you, that when you come through the door called Christ Jesus, things are supposed to work out for you. The reason a lot of things are not working out in the lives of most Christians is simply because we don't expect them to or believe they will. The reason a lot of things do not get better and we are not experiencing life-changing come-throughs and breakthroughs in our lives is because, in most cases, life experiences have taught us not to expect them to. In a lot of ways, we have accepted that this way that we have chosen in Christ and been chosen by Christ to live is inherent with going through with suffering and with not having. BUT THE BIBLE BEGS TO DIFFER. However, if you have Christ Jesus, your expectations must change. This does not mean trouble will not come, but it does mean that for every trial, every trouble, every disturbance, God has already provided a way of escape. There is not a trial that can worry you, that can befall you that God has not already worked out an escape for that is acceptable unto him. MARVELOUS THINGS! It is of utmost importance that the people of God eat this concept and digest this understanding and walk out this revelation. Trouble will come. Offenses will come. Things will happen, unexpected things, unexplainable things. But the Word of God says that Jesus is the door and once we come through the door called Jesus, he is going to turn us out to pasture. What kind of pasture? Green pastures. IT IS ALL RIGHT TO BE BLESSED. IT IS ALL RIGHT TO BE HAPPY. IT IS ALL RIGHT FOR THINGS TO WORK OUT TO YOUR FAVOR. Having much or doing well is not an indication of not being saved or knowing the Lord. Suffering is not indicative of being a child of God. You can and you should be genuinely happy, and your relationship with God be wonderfully and perfectly intact. The enemy has fooled many of us into believing that being saved means being lonely or that being saved is just indicative of not having a job or that being broke is just a part of being a child of God. "Suffering for the sake of Christ"—the devil is a liar! Everything you need is in Christ Jesus; therefore, the people of God must increase their expectation, even on what life is going to bring forth on their behalf. We find that many of us are simply living beneath our privilege, in Christ, or we just simply fail to have prevailing faith in the trials or transitions of life. The powers of darkness come to tell us that we "deserve where we find ourselves in life because we don't deserve better." These powers work to put the child of the Living God in a place where he/she has become accepting of where they find themselves and comfortable with living beneath their privilege, in Christ Jesus. Therefore, we are left not expecting more because we do not believe it is in the Father's will that we accomplish more for, by, and through him. The true revelation here is that none of us that have deserve what we have. We have because of the grace of God that has been shared "us-ward."

"For in him we live, and move, and have our being; as certain also of your own poets have said, for we are also his offspring" (Acts 17:28).

Truly, we find ourselves where we are as a result of our reliance and trust on God for his grace to dictate the flow of his evidences in our lives. Why won't you believe God? You are not so bad that God can't save you, that God can't deliver you, that God can't turn your life in a direction that your past did not dictate. Oftentimes, our faith lends itself to believing God for our deliverance or our healing, but we just will not believe God to bless us beyond what we fathom we deserve. We will give God praise because as we put it, "we were healed by his grace," or we did not deserve it. We will give God glory because we explain, "it was by God's grace" that we were delivered. But we will not believe in our hearts and therefore receive by the Spirit in our spirits, that by his grace we can be blessed. And it is in this type of thinking that we come to realize why doors do not readily open on our behalf, simply because we do not believe God for more. Triumphant living! It is clear that Jesus did not come in the flesh for the believer to remain the tail or on the bottom or rejected and dejected; it is a matter of fact that Jesus took the form and manner in which he came so we, his people, would not have to. We, as the people of God, have got to believe God for more, and we have got to begin to rebut life itself when it does not line up with our understanding of what God's will is as it pertains to his purpose for us. It is not okay to be broke. Stop allowing the enemy to tell you that it is just a consequence of being saved. Stop chunking up not having or not being happy to just being saved. These things are just synonymous with your relationship with Christ. Actually, things are the tricks of Satan, designed to separate God's people from the abundance that is found in him. God is more than able, by faith, to bless us beyond these type of situations or circumstances. Never quantify your worth in Christ by the amount of suffering you endure. It is a dangerous proposition that blinds you from the glory of God and the goodness that he has in store for you. Just because the enemy steals and takes from you on a continual basis does not qualify you as deep in the things of Christ. The devil is a liar, a murderer, and a thief, and he will extort from you what you allow him to.

Make up in your mind even now that you are going to take a stand in the spirit. Take a stand that says everything that God said was yours in the Holy Spirit, that you are going to take him for his word, that you are going to believe God for it. Regardless of your past. egardless of the things you may have done or been a part of or the mistakes you have made. You must take God for his word. The word he has spoken in your spirit that is stuck somewhere in your knowledge. Those things that you cannot quite put your finger on because you can't see them but you know deep down that they are true. At the root of your disappointment for where you are is an understanding of what should be. That was a gift from God to your Spirit Man. Under the right circumstances and guidance, this now would be hope and fuel to guide you to your future and God's plan for your life. But left unattended and unfulfilled, the enemy transforms it and perverts it to look more like despair and depression. So there again; regardless of what has transpired in the past, approach God and make it known that you will not be lazy and if he would show you what he would have you to do, you will do it.

> Then said Jesus unto them again, Verily, verily, I say unto you, I am the door of the sheep. All that ever came before me are thieves and robbers: but the sheep did not hear them. I am the door: by me if any man enters in, he shall be saved, and shall go in and out, and find pasture. (John 10:7–9)

Here, the Master is explaining that any man that comes unto him will go in and out, out and into pasture. He is not referring to the hereafter, but he is referring to the now. Wherever his feet shall trod, he is going to find the blessed things of God. If we are not finding this, the issue is not with Jesus, but the issue is with us and our approach to his Word. No, we are not going through because we are saved, and in a lot of ways, our approach to that notion is a mental mechanism that allows us to cope with what we do not understand. But believe me when I tell you the devil is a liar and in Christ Jesus, there is abundant living. Matthew 19:29 says, "And every one that hath forsaken houses, or brethren, or sisters, or father, or mother, or wife, or children, or lands, for my name's sake, shall receive a hundredfold, and shall inherit everlasting life."

This saying reflects the blessings of God on this side of everlasting life. The reason we continue to experience personal loss is because we accept our present state and fail to demand our inheritance in Christ to be made evident in our lives. It is the true nature of a robber to continue his assault until a demand is made for him to stop his extortion based out of some level of his dealings being exposed. Only when in your mind you have had a fundamental change that says, "I don't believe this. I don't believe I deserve this. I am a child of the King," does the enemy halt his assault because of the demand on your inheritance in Christ being made by your faith in him. The reason for distinct pockets in the body of Christ that have experienced the increase in personal wealth as they increased in faith is because of their willingness to believe and their acceptance of gospel truths that many of the gospel technicians began to teach across the country. All due to mind-set changes that in time influenced the balance of control in the spirit realm. In the Old Time Holiness (denomination) churches, it was commonly expressed that going through and not having was synonymous with being a child of God. It was also said that, if you were not going through, it was because you were not living worth anything. The devil is a liar. A lie from hell and we have accepted it in many ways in the body of Christ.

This is the equivalent of believing that unless a body is sick, it is not alive or to predicate that to be well is to experience sudden death. We have it so ingrained in our psyches that if things are presuming to go well for us, we get nervous, almost as to say if things are going good, something is wrong. Why not the other way around? If things are not going well, something is wrong.

Reflect on King David. No matter where he was found, God prepared a table before him. Ezekiel—even in his valley of dry bones, God took care of him. These great men of God were not pitiful in their happenstances, but they were settled in who they were and never lost focus on the promises of God that resided in their bellies. It is impossible to name one assured person of God who was pitiful in their circumstances. Not one called-out person of God. No matter where they found themselves in life, once they understood and accepted their place in life, they were okay mentally and spiritually, and they did not struggle with their God identity. But we make the fatal mistake of struggling with who we are. We fight with where we are because all the time we have not gotten a true understanding of who God is. So the enemy comes and fools us by telling us, "Every time you get something, you are supposed to lose it." And because in so many ways that is what we believe, we fail to properly utilize the power of prayer. The truth of the matter is, you will not fight for what you do not believe is yours. So we are faced with a combination of the ignorance of how to employ the weapons of our warfare and a laziness to engage in the activities that are necessary to employ them. So we began the process of preparing ourselves to lose before we lose. We prepare our minds and those around us by saying, "To God be the glory." There is no glory for God in the enemy taking advantage of his people. There is no glory for God in a testimony of his blessing in an area and then another eventual testimony of you losing that very same thing in the very same area of your testimony. There is no glory there; the devil is a liar. The scripture declares in Luke 9: 62, "And Jesus said unto him, no man, having put his hand to the plough, and looking back, is fit for the kingdom of God."

Our God is a God of progression, not a God of oppression, suppression, or depression. The greater revelation here is, as the scripture declares, since the days of the prophet, the kingdom has suffered violence, and the violence has taken it by force. RESISTANCE is the key. Look at James 4:7–10

> Submit yourselves therefore to God. Resist the devil, and he will flee from you. Draw nigh to God, and he will draw nigh to you. Cleanse your hands, ye sinners; and purify your hearts, ye double minded. Be afflicted, and mourn, and weep: let your laughter be turned to mourning, and your joy to heaviness. Humble yourselves in the sight of the Lord, and he shall lift you up.

Before you give up, get tougher in the spirit. Before you let go, tighten up your grip. Before you allow the enemy to pervert what you said the Lord gave you by faith, formulate a willingness to war in the spirit for what you know is yours. Grace afforded you to have much of what you have, but your faith and stance in God is what will afford you to keep it. But a nonchalant attitude towards losing what God has given you is never acceptable to him. Some things are supposed to provoke you to action in the Spirit of God. Not an attitude that says, "Everybody knows how it is," or "This way is a hard way," or "We as Christians suffer." The devil is a liar.

Think about Peter and the disciples when they came to Jesus and told him that it was noised that they needed to pay their taxes. Jesus did not respond with a statement that sounded like, "Everybody knows that we are trying to make it," or "This way is a hard way," but he said in Matthew 17:27, "Notwithstanding, lest we should offend them, go thou to the sea, and cast a hook, and take up the fish that first cometh up; and when thou hast opened his mouth, thou shalt find a piece of money: that take, and give unto them for me and thee."

Jesus made it clear that it was not acceptable to not properly represent the kingdom of God with what was expected in the kingdom of men. In the spirit, Jesus ministered that before you let up, tighten up. Before you give up on the needs brought to bare by insufficiency in the natural, tighten up your faith in God to make way for a supernatural intervention. When things are not available for you in the natural, start reaching out in the spirit for it is there that the things that are eventually seen are manifested from. But whatever you do, don't give up. Don't just offer an excuse that soothes the mind but does nothing to win the victory. Remember, you never have to have what you need at a given time in your pocket because you are a signer on God's account. By faith, you can write a check on God's account and expect to cash it. God's account never runs short. You have the power through and by the Holy Spirit to work your way out of whatever condition you find yourself in, all in the name of Jesus. "And all things, whatsoever ye shall ask in prayer, believing, ye shall receive" (Matthew 21:22). How powerful is that?

So with all this in mind, we understand that we live where our faith affords us to live, not our job. We drive what our faith allows us to drive, not our credit alone. Of course, there is a level of knowledge and understanding that must accompany this thought, but the fact still remains that it is true. According to your faith, be it done unto you. So it is impossible for me to look at you and not see your faith.

If you are not living where the Spirit of the Lord agrees within you that you should live, then you must somehow, someway, believe God for more. Your faith must increase beyond what you perceive to be possible at this given time. Romans 8:24–25 says, "For we are saved by hope: but hope that is seen is not hope: for what a man seeth, why doth he yet hope for? But if we hope for that we see not, then do we with patience wait for it."

Hence, faith is not what you see, yet faith is what you dare hope beyond what present circumstances dictates. It has nothing to do with what you have because if you had it, you would not have a need to hope for it. We must believe before we have a reason to. We must believe short of the evidence. Once you believe to the evidence, you must believe beyond it. We are all in different places in faith. To every man, there has been given a measure of faith. So you believe according to your faith and the grace given unto you to believe. Some are believing just short of where they are going. Some are standing in the place where your anemic faith has brought them, and they must start believing God for faith beyond where they are. However, no one has room to be complacent as it relates to their faith. Jesus spoke of his purpose in God as he was being led up Golgotha's hill, saying, "Do not weep for me."

Jesus simply implied that he still had his dignity because he was on course with his purpose in the Father. We all must thrive to acquire the next level in God as it pertains to our faith in him. Some might respond that they are believing God but nothing is moving. This simply means you have hit a wall and there is nothing to do about a wall standing between your faith and your purpose but knock it down. HOW DO I KNOCK IT DOWN? Well, this kind goes only by fasting and praying. We must first know what the weapons of our warfare are, and then we must have the courage and fortitude to employ them. Do you believe it? First of all, do you believe everything the Holy Spirit has ministered to you concerning who you are, and secondly, do you believe the Word of God concerning how to walk in it? Do you believe it? One of the best ways to increase your ability to believe God for who he says you are in him is to surround yourself with believers and people of faith who inspire you to believe. Your faith will reflect that of the company that you keep. Be numbered with those who have great faith. Excuse yourself from the company of the naysayers in your life. Partner with people who are on the move for God, and through association, your faith will grow. One of the best things that could have ever happened to Silas was his connection with Paul. Silas was blessed through that association. Paul and Silas were drawn together as a result of strange circumstances, but the pairing was unquestionably the work of God. Yoke with people who can help pull you up to the next level in Christ. If you place a pitiful-minded person in a beautiful predicament, they will not stay there, and by the same token, if you place a faithful, upbeat believer in a hole, he will not stay there, and the upward or downward movement has everything to do with the individual's approach to God. There is a premium in knowing who God is and having faith in what God can do. Mary the sister of Lazarus did not know a lot about the deeper things of God; however, she knew the value of sitting at Jesus's feet and being bathed by the anointing of the words that flowed from his mouth. I would say she did not understand everything that Jesus had to say, but she allowed the anointing to just run down on her. And it was the anointing, not her understanding of words, that changed her life. "'Not by Power, nor by Might, but by his Spirit,' sayeth the Lord" (Zechariah 4:6). Take time now, and repeat aloud. "I bind up the spirits that come that cause me to feel sorry for myself." Speak an open declaration over your life that the next time the urge to feel sorrow for yourself comes, that the inclination will not rest well with you and your supernatural response will be to bind up the spirits that carried the notion. Feeling sorry for yourself is beneath you simply because you do not have to stand there empty-handed. You do not have to stand there as though you are helpless. With Christ Jesus, you are never alone, and you are never helpless. The Bible offers Samson as one of the examples of strength to the believer.

Judges 15:15 offers that when attacked by the Philistines, Samson looked up and realized that he was surrounded by

Philistines. At that moment, Samson did not worry nor was he overcome by a sense of helplessness for he knew that he had the power to overcome. He knew that all he needed was the tool to funnel the power through. Immediately, he surveyed the present area he found himself in, and to God be the glory, he saw the "new" jawbone of an ass lying on the ground. The significance of the jawbone being new is of paramount proportion. *New* implies that it was freshly supplied and of the *divine providence*. It was up to Samson to realize that it was all he needed to get the job done. With the jawbone, Samson slew a thousand men. In his vigor, he was able to keep them in front of him and never allowed them to get behind him. He was outnumbered but never surrounded. Fortitude in God will give you the vision to see hope against insurmountable odds. Samson's faith in God, his trust in his ability, and his willingness to fight won him the day. Samson surmised that he had the power, he had the ability, and all he needed was something in his hand. He inherently knew that the trial he was facing was beneath the anointing that was on his life. He knew that the call of God on his life was greater than what he was facing. He looked at the situation in its totality and said, "Not like this." He thought the situation to be beneath him and willed himself to victory by the gift of God that was in him. He never looked at the numbers in terms of individuals. He never saw individuals; he saw the Philistines. If he would have studied the individual men that made up his overall problem, he would have been overwhelmed. But the thought processes of a triumphant-living person are different from those of a victim of life. The triumphant-living person surmises the attack and the individual components of the attack. Instead of fighting a thousand small battles, Samson fought one big battle and won. Satan is a liar, and he masters the art of distraction. If he can distract your attention by his methods of overwhelming you with a constant blast of trials, he never has to concern himself with you warring in the Spirit against adversity as a whole in your life. When we dissect our problems, oftentimes, we become overwhelmed by the magnitude of the different aspects that make up the problem. Afterwards, Samson was sorely thirsty. Samson went from an outward attack directly to an inward attack. His thirst was a thirst that brought him to the point of death. But he recalled his testimony of how great a thing God had done for him and once again refused to believe that such a thing as thirst could defeat him. Faith must be founded or anchored by a core belief. Samson knew that God was at the center of his strength and his abilities. He knew that God was the essence of who he was and the center of his joy. He understood that outside of his ability in God, he was nothing; he was average at best. So he relied on his ability to tap into God. What is your mental picture that reflects your approach to your Spiritual God? Who is he, and what is he in your life? What are you using to help you draw your conclusions about him? The best way to approach these questions is to go back and take an account of the parts he has already played in the successes of your life. Just as we have expectations of God, he has expectations of us, and at the core of his expectations of us is that we trust him. Remember, in your weakness, he is made strong. Look at our scripture, John 10:10, "The thief cometh not, but for to steal, and to kill, and to destroy: I am come that they might have life, and that they might have it more abundantly."

    Satan has no purpose in the lives of men other than this. However, Jesus explains that his purpose is not to take or make you sick or tear you down. That's Satan's job. Jesus proclaims that he came that we might have life and live that life on a level beyond possible before his coming. This verse makes it clear that trials are not happening to you just because you are saved or because you love God so well. Anything outside of a trying of your faith is the hand of Satan in your life. The Scriptures tell us that the people of God perish due to lack of knowledge. It is in these gray areas of not knowing that the enemy thrives, lurks, and takes full advantage of the people of God. Satan works in the mind of the believer to covertly pass his detrimental attributes over to our Lord and Savior in the mind of the believer. All of this is in an effort to raise questions in the mind of the believer over the knowledge of God that lives there.

We, as the people of God, must learn to war against our own nature. Honestly speaking, many of us, before accepting Christ into our lives, had hang-ups that were detrimental to success. Laziness, trifle, low self-esteem, low self-confidence just to name a few. If we do not seek the Lord to be born of the Spirit as well as the water, that old mindset will taint every effort we engage in, even after yielding to the call of Christ. There is a natural part of a man that causes him to be who he is at the core that has nothing to do with the Spirit until that man learns to yield those hidden places in himself. The difficult part about yielding these places is, without the guidance of the Holy Spirit, the individual may not even know that these trapdoors of the mind that open to the deficiencies of the psychology of a man even exist. We did not wait to get saved to deal with depression. Many of us dealt with depression before salvation. Many of us spent exorbitant amounts of time not managing our time and engaged in non-productive activities, and now that we are saved, we exhibit many of the same lazy approaches to what we say we need God to do for us. The key to escaping here is found in being born again and continuous deliverance. Your next move in God is all about your understanding of who Jesus is and what he came to do.

The Bible says that the power of life and death is in the tongue, so no matter what the issue, you can speak life and live. If and when you speak life, as a child of God on any front, be the topic, natural or spiritual. Be assured that through and by the power of God channeled by your faith, life must come. How will you speak it? "From the abundance of the heart, the mouth speaketh" (Luke 6:45). You cannot speak with power what is not in you. And what's in you only becomes a part of you by faith. If you can walk where you are and if that place is less desirable than what you perceive is purposed by God for your life, you can speak life by faith on a continual basis. Be open for a move and an interjection by the Holy Spirit. Be prepared to do what he instructs you to do, and you will receive a life-changing move of God. The "to do" is the key here simply because you must be prepared to do or follow the instructions laid out by the Holy Spirit. Many are prepared to hear; however, they are not stimulated by faith enough to do. God is moved by faith, and he builds your faith at every encounter. God's motive is that he loves you, and his method is to systematically drive you to your ultimate purpose in him. That's why in him, one cause feeds another action and so on and so forth. In your weakness, he is made strong, and his joy is your strength. Fear is a mental block set up by Satan that will hinder the manifestation of faith in the believer that motivates him to doing. The fear of the unknown, knowing too much concerning the current situation, unfamiliarity with where God is leading you, unwillingness to trust God by stepping out on faith. We are not in control of the times of our lives. But by not releasing the faith necessary to sanction the next move of God that he has ordained in our lives, we can certainly make a mess of it.

Jesus said, "I am come that they might have life and that they might have it more abundantly. I have come that you might not be tormented, that you might not be robbed, that you might not be taken advantage of." Jesus came not just to give us life naturally, because by the time a thing becomes evident in the natural, it has been in existence for a long time in the spirit. That's one of the things so awesome about being saved, because by walking with God and being led by his Spirit, he allows you to escape the tempter's snares. So a lot of things the enemy set out to do come to naught in your life because the hand of God destroys them before they even manifest in the natural. Abundant living also implies on more levels than previously experienced. To be able to experience the fullness of life on more levels. That they may better understand the richness of life. God is revealing through his Word that there is a depth to the breath of life that he wants his people to learn to enjoy. God wants his people to know him in the beauty of holiness. God does not desire us to just know him in death, but he wants us to know him on earth. Freely loving God through the dictates of your faith and he would freely love you in the sweetness of your choice. That's why we worship, and that's why we praise, because we know him. When trouble comes and when trials come, we do not lose who we are in God. Our mental projection of our Spiritual God is such that you are sustained in the lean times for you have come to realize that he is life in the presence of death. Faith affords opportunities. No, I am not referring to magical or mystical occurrences here, but the Holy Spirit will speak to you, for his core competency is to bring faith to pass. He will instruct you on the lines of what you are believing him for. He will aid you in the sustainability of your faith by instructing you by his Spirit as you move along the road of your purpose. Be certain to work to sustain your belief in who you are in him. To know who God is but to have no concept of who you are in God is a failing proposition. This is a crucial piece as you work to revamp your approach to being blessed. Many of us are working to be built up in faith as to who God is. However, we fail to understand that what God does for us, he is more than likely going to perform through us. Your understanding of who you are in him is almost as important as knowing who he is. Think back on the scriptures. Abraham was made to know, Gideon was made to know, Moses was made to know, and you and I will be made to know. That's why purposeful trials are a trying of your faith. They make you better. They make you stronger. They work together for your good. Certainly, it is not the trial that makes you stronger in faith but understanding what you suffered and learning from the experience. Of course, true increase will be measured by, at some point, coming out of the trial with a testimony of God's goodness and power. In this faith, when we enter into a trial and over stay the trial, the opposite effect occurs. We become weary in the faith, and eventually, we lose our testimony. It's the equivalent of being in a hailstorm and not getting any breaks in the clouds. That's not God. There is no God purpose to your trial, and faith is the only thing to be gained in those types of assaults by the enemy. It is your testimony that gives you the strength to believe. True testimony, which is the essence of God's glory, is not made evident until you come through. You have got to come out at some point if it is God, because he came that you might have life and that you might have IT more abundantly.

God wants us multifaceted as it relates to our faith in him. Simply, approaching the things of God from a black-or-white standpoint is not his perfect will for his people. God wants complexity in our relationships with him, and he will be whatever we take him to be. There are and can be shades of gray, green, yellow, blue, red, and all the colors of the spectrum in the magnificent splendor of the possibilities in God. Limited faith will guarantee a broken-down, poor-mouthed, can't-get-a-move, haven't-seen-God, have-you-seen-God relationship with him, limited by your constrictions on faith. Faith needs to be free to take form under the direction of the Holy Spirit according to the designed purpose for your life. Predetermined faith will hinder the flow of God's designed purpose for your life.

But he has said, "Life more abundantly." He says, "I want to give you more revelations concerning who I am. I want to give you more revelations concerning who you are in me." It is God's will that you come through, out of, and over every obstacle life has to offer. It is God's good pleasure that you experience triumphant living on this side of heaven. What are you expecting? Are you willing to do? When God speaks to me by his Spirit, I will do what he tells me to do. I will war against those things that come natural to me if they are not conducive to a move of God in my life. Learn to do on shaky faith. Your faith does not have to be rock solid for you to move out and do. It is not the size of the faith that moves mountains but the amount of faith necessary to say; God has promised to do the heavy lifting if we would dare say! Mustard seed faith. The type of faith that leads you to a verb (action). The strength of mustard seed faith is the belief that you can say to the mountain, "Be thou removed." However; the stimulant that provokes God is when you GO and say to the mountain. We cannot complain about what God has not done if our faith has not prompted us to move out and do something beyond WAIT, if we have not been moved to prepare a resume and start the process of filling out applications. Faith without works is dead faith or faith without any hope of motivating God to perform as a result of our notion. Do! Do! When you believe God and you do, it is a dare to God, and he will prove himself, his wonders to perform.

# The Power to Overcome Catastrophe

It is important at the outset of this chapter to grasp an understanding that says, "What God has purposed to do in your life, no one can do but him." Certainly, the Power to Overcome Catastrophe is an anointing that will allow you to outlast the devil's onslaught against you, whatever that might be. There is an anointing that will allow you to stand beyond whatever it is the enemy is confronting you with. One of the most awesome places in the Lord to find yourself is in a place where you have a combination of the anointing and patience. There are a lot of Christians who are anointed but are lacking in patience. Patience is a derivative of faith. Your anointing, no matter how great, is of less consequence when patience is not present. Patience is the thought that is contrived from an understanding of what is implied by the definition of faith in the Word of God.

> "Now faith is the substance of things hoped for, the evidence of things not seen" (Hebrews 11:1).

Patience can serve as evidence of things not seen. Patience speaks to your behavior. Patience is not just sitting silently, but patience speaks to your response to the knowledge you have gathered as it concerns your position in life. It goes beyond what has been spoken. It goes beyond what you have understood at any given time concerning what God's will is for your life. It speaks to very real situations, very real issues, that we find ourselves in. Your response to where you find yourself speaks to your level of patience and, ultimately, your faith. Anointing plus patience will equate to a come-through for those who possess them both. I purposely did not say *breakthrough* here because before you can BREAK through, you must COME through. Breakthrough is the ultimate in moving from one level of life and spiritual aptitude to another. Come-through speaks to a horizontal move across a given level that allows you to flow progressively on that level to reach the fullness of that purpose, for the level, as designed by God. Where you are going has already been predetermined; you have just got to get there. Some of the instances in our walk with God we are calling breakthroughs are not really breakthroughs but are actually come-throughs. We have an uncanny knack in the body of Christ for overstating our position in life relative to God's purpose for us because we understate the possibilities in Christ Jesus for our lives. We attribute the reclamation of property or reclaiming things of old, stolen from us by the devil and confiscated for us by the Holy Spirit as new heights in God, when actually, the levels have not changed but we have simply, by the grace of God, have been allowed to reclaim ground lost on the same level we were on. Acquiring the money to pay your light bill is not a breakthrough, simply because God knew you would need the money before the bill was due. However, Satan, through whatever means, has deployed slothfulness and lack of faith, ambushed, and stole the provisions that God had made. COME THROUGH! BREAKTHROUGH! This is when God elevates you by his Spirit in your faith to a point where your faith in him propels you to a place in him where your physical condition changes and you no longer have bill-paying issues. You have got to last long enough to come through. Your reward for coming through is breaking through.

It is important to note that all undesirable places in life are not catastrophes. Catastrophes are those situations and circumstances that come up oftentimes out of nowhere that cause the flow of your life to come to a screeching halt. Those occurrences that come have the potential to turn your life upside down and to totally take you out of the flow of what you understand is God's purpose for your life. These are the times that are sent to make shipwreck and to change the very nomenclature of your life. A mess. Something that is detrimental. Something perceived by you if not by anyone else. It can be relegated to your mind, body, or the spirit. It is when you come to a place or a point where you cannot get out unless the hand of God rescues you. Look at Acts 20:1-12.

> And after the uproar was ceased, Paul called unto him the disciples, and embraced them, and departed for to go into Macedonia. And when he had gone over those parts, and had given them much exhortation, he came into Greece, and there abode three months. And when the Jews laid wait for him, as he was about to sail into Syria, he purposed to return through Macedonia. And there accompanied him into Asia Sopater of Berea; and of the Thessalonians, Aristarchus and Secundus; and Gaius of Derbe, and Timotheus; and of Asia, Tychicus and Trophimus. These going before tarried for us at Troas. And we sailed away from Philippi after the days of unleavened bread, and came unto them to Troas in five days; where we abode seven days. And upon the first day of the week, when the disciples came together to break bread, Paul preached unto them, ready to depart on the morrow; and continued his speech until midnight. And there were many lights in the upper chamber, where they were gathered together. And there sat in a window a certain young man named Eutychus, being fallen into a deep sleep: and as Paul was long preaching, he sunk down with sleep, and fell down from the third loft, and was taken up dead. And Paul went down, and fell on him,

and embracing him said, Trouble not yourselves; for his life is in him. When he therefore was come up again, and had broken bread, and eaten, and talked a long while, even till break of day, so he departed. And they brought the young man alive, and were not a little comforted.

Paul is going about the work of the ministry, taking every opportunity to share the gospel. One very obvious result of the ministry of Paul was that wherever Paul ministered one of two things would always be the result. Either he was received and many were saved and enlightened, or his life would be threatened and he would be on the run to preserve it. Paul oftentimes met opposition. On many occasions, people will serve as that opposition. It is important to note that people will come up against you as you go about the business of fulfilling your purpose in Christ Jesus. This is no catastrophe; it is just the reality of who we are and what we do. Never allow the enemy to confuse in your mind the true state of things. Certain aspects of who you are and what you are becoming in the Lord are inherent with not being understood or isolation. Consistently walking in your calling will alleviate a great deal of the not being understood and feeling of isolation in time. Paul's example for us here is, never allow the opposition to stop you from doing and being who you know you have been purposed to be. So with that said, in his stance and his determinate manner, Paul perseveres without ever taking an account that is what he is doing. He is intensely focused on the rudiments of his purpose to the point that the work blinds him of the uniqueness of his struggles. He is so busy climbing out of the hole that he does not take the time to survey the vastness of the ditch. He gives his faith every opportunity to succeed by his approach to the unfolding events all around him. Hallelujah! He perseveres right through the trials and trouble to claim the greatness that has been stored up for him. One triumph at a time. From glory to glory. Before it is all said and done, Paul will write thirteen epistles and go on to be one of the greatest preachers of all time, but before he can, he must first survive the Book of Acts.

We see here that Paul had learned to accept opposition as a way of life. Paul learned early on in his ministry that he was not called to strive against opposition. If you spend the better part of your time striving against opposition, you will find yourself diverted from your true mission in the spirit, diverted from the true call of God in your life. Only consistency can win over people, and if you are consistently doing the work of the Lord and what you have been called to do, the evidence of your dedication will, in time, win over your harshest critics. One of the most valuable lessons to learn from Paul here is the lesson of perseverance. Paul accepted the fact that opposition was a part of his calling. He stopped being surprised when people or groups of people would not accept his teaching and come up against him. When you understand how important it is to stay focused on the plan, you will ultimately achieve the dictates of the plan. Paul understood that when he accepted Christ, that it was God who he belonged to from that day forward. Paul was so understanding of this fact that he did not hold people accountable when they did not understand his philosophy or his level of dedication as it pertained to the Lord. Paul understood full well that his God experiences made him special. He did not expect everyone to approach his vision of Jesus in the same manner in which he had. He understood that his proximity to the move of God afforded him to be the teacher, and his task was not only to teach but to introduce all he came across with in his travels to Jesus Christ. Paul did not change his position in God every time someone disagreed with him. Paul did not get upset when people did not want him around or asked him to leave. He understood that, that was the common reaction he got from people and that it was not to him but to the strong anointing of God that was on his life. Paul's knowledge of God and the effect that he had on people afforded him to not take the reactions of people personal. We could be so much more for

God if we would learn this lesson from Paul and not take things so personal.

Paul was powerful, and wherever he could find room to preach, he would preach. Whenever he found people who would hear what he had to say, he would expound. Whenever he would run into people who did not want to hear him, he never lost sleep; he never made those matters topics of conversation because he knew how important it was for his Spirit Man to stay free. As you read the Book of Acts, you find that Paul and the apostles have adopted an attitude that simply says, "We are going on with Jesus." Every episode, whether good or bad, was considered just another event on the road to fulfilling their purpose in God. These men refused to allow the things that occurred that were less favorable to hinder them in their plight to please God. They understood that they were on God's time. They focused on the positives. Look at Acts 20:7–12.

> And upon the first day of the week, when the disciples came together to break bread, Paul preached unto them, ready to depart on the morrow; and continued his speech until midnight. And there were many lights in the upper chamber, where they were gathered together. And there sat in a window a certain young man named Eutychus, being fallen into a deep sleep: and as Paul was long preaching, he sunk down with sleep, and fell down from the third loft, and was taken up dead. And Paul went down, and fell on him, and embracing him said, Trouble not yourselves; for his life is in him. When he therefore was come up again, and had broken bread, and eaten, and talked a long while, even till break of day, so he departed. And they brought the young man alive, and were not a little comforted.

Preaching was a customary event for Paul; this was his way. There was nothing strange about Paul preaching the word of God to believers as well as nonbelievers. Preaching all night was something Paul could do because of the abundance of revelatory word that was in him. Paul was free to walk in the gifts of God. So while the others broke bread, Paul preached. Paul was totally unaffected by rejection. Paul was full of the anointing of the Holy Spirit and had no real way to turn the anointing off, on, or down. Paul preached until past midnight and into the next day. It is not clear if the brethren were having a good time, but it is clear that Paul was. The anointing of God and the Spirit of God is a foot. No doubt being that there is a room of preachers there; the gospel that is being expounded upon is a rich gospel full of fresh revelatory knowledge. So Paul was speaking on the deeper things of God, and the atmosphere was charged with the anointing of the Holy Spirit. Most everybody in the room was actively engaged with the anointing and presentation of the Holy Spirit in their midst at that moment and in that very hour; what God would have happening is transpiring in that place. When you find yourself in the place where God would have you be, doing what God would have you doing, experiencing exactly what God would have you experience, you find yourself in that "perfect" place in God. In that place where God is blessing, when God is revealing himself, and there is no better place to be found in God than when he is revealing himself to his children. When God reveals himself to you, it increases your faith; it increases your ability to please him. When God reveals himself, he oftentimes will have something said in your midst that you may never have heard before, but it agrees with you in your spirit, as if you had known it but never could put words to it. There is no greater blessing than a "fresh" revelation about the Father. That revelation makes a better Christian and soldier for the Lord out of you. That revelation will inspire you to go and try and achieve things you never would have tried before. Paul was sharing that type of revelatory knowledge.

It is important to note that the unleashing of revelatory knowledge is an affront to the enemy, and he majors in disrupting levels of knowledge that bring life to the hearers. The rulers of darkness hate it when the people of God are on the right accord in the Spirit and are spiritually and harmonically tuned to the proper frequency to receive a word prone to birth breakthroughs in the lives of the hearers. So distraction is often the tool of choice that the enemy will employ to remove the people of God from this very delicate place in God. First of all, it is no small feat to get in this very special place, and it is an even more difficult one to stay there. Satan seeks distraction to change the very nomenclature of the atmosphere. Spiritually, the enemy cannot afford for you to spend great lengths of time in this place. We, as the people of God, must seek the Lord's face for an anointing so we can refuse to allow Satan to change the atmosphere around us (the power to overcome catastrophe). God has a greater blessing for his people, but we must study to have the mind of Jesus and Paul. We must study to have the heart of Jesus and Paul, the mental toughness brought about by faith to outlast the blast and stay functional in Christ throughout the process. Paul was the type of individual in God who could walk over speed bumps without ever looking down. See, Paul anticipated the speed bumps and adjusted his gait in the spirit to compensate for the occasion where they might be there. Trouble did not faze him because he refused to allow the devil to dictate to him what season he was in, in his ministry, his life, or his walk with Jesus Christ. He refused to allow the powers of darkness to interrupt his season of joy and exhortation with catastrophe. God has given us the power through our faith in Christ Jesus to overcome catastrophe. A terrible and awful thing in life, hurtful things, life-shaping, and life-changing things, God has given us the power to overcome. The powers of darkness are always seeking to get in the midst of your "service" and rename what type it is. They are always seeking methods to redefine your season by their own terms. Satan wants to change your season from joy to sadness. He wants to change your marriage ceremony into a funeral. He wants to turn your rejoicing into sorrow. But when you are in the Spirit, you have the authority by the Holy Spirit, which is activated by the anointing and your patience in the Lord. A calmness that is brought about by your confidence in God and directed by your faith straight to the heart of the issue that the enemy is working to spring forth. An anointing that refuses to be dealt with but is well prepared to deal with the tricks of the enemy. The anointing and the patience to come through. Wherever you find yourself as you read this, I speak a word directly to your Spirit Man that says, "COME THROUGH!"

According to this scripture, in the midst of this great revelatory move of God, Satan sought to put the meeting in a state of panic, uproar, and horror. Satan loves to stand in a corner and scream "Fire!" so he can watch the people of God trip all over themselves trying to escape what they have through the power of Christ Jesus to extinguish. He loves it when we take his word for the end of a thing without validating the situation with Jesus, who is the author and finisher of our faith. Satan is always working to change the flow of God in the midst of his people. That's his job! Through the Spirit of God, we will be able to both discern and anticipate the influence of Satan on a given situation. The scripture makes it clear that the lights were on; it was not dark in the hall. Yet and still, Eutychus fell into a deep sleep. How? Sitting in a window (fresh air) and a lot of lights. The Word also informs us that he was a young man, not old, yet he fell asleep and eventually fell to his death. Nothing but the devil. The powers of darkness were looking for an opportunity to introduce catastrophe into the gathering. Satan desired to turn this meeting into a catastrophe. The gifts of knowledge, wisdom, and discernment will help you recognize when the enemy is working to make a mess of your season in God. A catastrophe in the making, Paul keeps preaching, and Eutychus keeps nodding off. No doubt this went on for quite some time, until at the moment the enemy determined most opportune, Eutychus came falling down from the third loft. Those around him picked him up dead, and as far as they were concerned, the service, the hour and the time, had been gravely changed and altered by this occurrence. It is important to note that time will yield to the greater anointing or display of faith in the immediate vicinity. How others perceived things was not the determining factor as to where this service went from here. It was Paul's ability to impress upon the reality of the moment, his faith for the future, that dictated the settled result of the present. Your first thoughts of your now does not have to be the testimony that gets birthed. As soon as Paul saw him, he fell down on him and verbally proclaimed what he spiritually desired. He did not hold a conversation with those who were in no position to dictate the moment to him. The men watched, and Paul reacted by faith. He then rebutted what the enemy had proclaimed by deed and said, "Trouble not yourselves for his life is in him." And it was so. Then I think Paul did what we all must be determined to do. **HE FINISHED WHAT HE HAD STARTED** before he was so rudely interrupted by the devil. Look at the eleventh verse of Acts 20, "When he therefore was come up again, and had broken bread, and eaten, and talked a long while, even till break of day, so he departed."

 The man of God averted the catastrophe by reactionary faith and a refusal to be moved by the designs of Satan. Think about it, as you go about your way talking about the goodness of Jesus Christ, proclaiming that Christ came that you might have life and life more abundantly, the enemy is seeking to give a very real show of the contradiction between the reality of what is happening in your life and what you are saying. His desire is to prove that as you speak life, death is what is most apparent.

 Now as catastrophic-type issues become apparent, many around you might respond with negativism or with a statement of the obvious, but remember to follow Paul's example: first steady yourself in Christ and refuse to be overtaken by fear, then stand up in the power of the might that God has given you through your faith in Christ Jesus, then speak those things that are not as though they were with an expectation of seeing what you speak. We, as the called of God, must stop allowing people to minister to us from a place in faith that is less than our revelation from God. We must lead in word and in deed. Refuse to allow what you see to overcome what you believe. Be driven by your understanding of your purpose. Not what you see, but your understanding of your purpose. That is why, ultimately, it is so important to know who you are in God. Who are you in the Lord? Offenses will come, but woe unto that man by whom offences come. Things will not always go according to plan, but you have been equipped by the Holy Spirit to make it out of whatever quick-sand you find yourself in, in life, and you must remain driven by your understanding of who you are in God. Refuse to believe that God is not true to his word. Never allow your faith to drop within you to a point where you reflect in countenance, word, or deed what the enemy is dictating. To say you believe is not enough, for when your countenance falls and when you began to reflect what has been dictated, then obviously, you have been affected by what has been stated. It is important not to be swayed by the feelings that are associated with hopelessness. Not to be touched by the inclination sent by the vipers of hell that say you are in a hopeless situation. Your faith will impose itself on your situation, and ultimately, through the passage of time, your faith and stance in God will win out over all else.

    Go back and reevaluate the trials you have come through, and you may find that the reason you are going through even now is because you are doing a marvelous job for the Lord, and that is why the enemy is coming up against you like a flood. Because when he comes up against you like a flood, our God will raise up a standard. In other words, God is going to do something in you. He is going to empower you. He is going to increase your grip on the things concerning him. There are different aspects of a man that are opened up to the enemy for trials designed to work patience and breed faith in the heart of the believer. But as we gain the wisdom for how to walk in the power that overcomes catastrophe, we will realize the victory on every level of our lives—spiritually, mentally, and physically. Remember the importance of staying focused on the promises of God and not allowing yourself to be distracted. War against the spirits of distraction, and refuse, through the battles of the mind and spirit, to allow the enemy to command your attention and focus. For as a man thinketh in his heart, so is he. When Satan possesses your mind, he has you. But there is power in knowing that the Lord of hope and grace has promised to keep you in perfect peace if you keep your mind stayed on him. Philippians 4:8 says, "Finally, brethren, whatsoever things are true, whatsoever things are honest, whatsoever things are just, whatsoever things are pure, whatsoever things are lovely, whatsoever things are of good report; if there be any virtue, and if there be any praise, think on these things."

This is how we break the hands of the enemy in our lives. Trouble will come, but never panic and never ever throw your hands up in aimless desperation, and never focus on what the enemy of all mankind is trying to show you. Focus your attention on your intent before trouble was made evident to you. If you were focused on the things concerning pleasing God, keep working for God for there is a powerful dispensation associated with your steadfastness in the things concerning him. Do know that God is establishing you through your steadfastness and your stance in the sight of all who are witnessing the outbreak of the dilemma. What God is about to prove about you in the midst of this issue will far outweigh anything you could dare say on your own behalf. I tell you that through the power that is found in Jesus Christ, through the authority that is given by the Holy Spirit, you have been given the power to overcome the catastrophes of your life. YOU WILL MAKE IT THROUGH AND OUT OF WHERE YOU AND YOURS CURRENTLY FIND YOURSELVES, in the name of Jesus. Never allow yourself to be overly affected by whatever effect the enemy is working to create. Bind up the sensation to dramatize the issues that are presented to you in the form of unexpected turns in life. Learn to downplay the obvious nature of unpleasant events. Drama is an enemy of hope and faith. Don't waddle in catastrophe by repeating and rehearsing the feeling connected to the initial impact or contact with the situation. Your reality will reflect what you are willing to accept as your outcome from any given input—input, being events and occurrences. Elevation in faith will allow you to get so high in the things of God that you see what is occurring but you don't see it, whereby your reaction is beyond your perception. When you look up and find yourself in the midst of a "hot mess," you must learn how to stay functional in the things of God. Folding arms and crying over the "hot messes" of life will not get them fixed. You must stay actively engaged in your place in God and ever be mindful of your purpose in him. That's when the weapons of our warfare, which are not carnal, come into play, and we begin to impose our faith on our issues. And while you are praising, testifying, praying, and fasting, you will look up and find that the "hot mess" would have long passed. Who are you in God, and even as important, who do you want to be? If you are in God, he is going to take care of you. No doubt about it. Trouble is going to come. Situations are going to come. But remember, you have the victory. The enemy has not been given the power to implement long-lasting effect in your life. The effect of the enemy in the life of a child of God is only for a season. To God be the glory! God is with you! Even in the midst of what you may be dealing with right this moment, God is with you! You just have to believe it and not give into the horrific nature of the moment. Fight to stay in the spirit. Don't allow the enemy to drag you off into the flesh. Weeping may endure for a night, but joy cometh in the morning.

# Blessed, Anointed, and Highly Favored

The blood of Jesus will never lose its power. There are three connotations that we will be discussing and addressing in this chapter: blessed, anointed, and highly favored. The Concept of Triumphant Living is one that embraces a different mindset and approach to life itself. It is to aspire in and through faith, to know God in the beauty of his holiness and, through this knowledge of who he is, gain a better understanding of who he desires for us to be. As we approach the main themes of this chapter, we must first visit two main topics that are directly connected to them. These two topics are very common in the body of Christ, and they serve to be pivotal in your well-being and success in both the Lord and in life in general. Salutations and benedictions are so common that we oftentimes take them for granted. Most of the time, because of how often we are involved with either of these concepts, we take for granted just how powerful and just how important and how impactful, in the spirit and otherwise, salutations and benedictions really are. Salutations and benedictions are so powerful, important, that they bare out that we should take time to gain more understanding as to what is actually occurring when we engage in salutations and benedictions. It is important to understand that either one of these activities are sacred decrees by faith, of things both present and things to come. Salutations and benedictions are acts of faith. A salutation is commonly viewed as a greeting used in a letter or other written or formal communication. They can be formal or informal. The most common form of salutation is the usage of "dear" in the opening stanzas of a letter. Even if the communication is unpleasant or even if the individual being addressed is not so "dear" to you, it is still customary to open with a salutation of dear—a wishful type of offering that eludes to things to come as a result of the communication at hand. It simply implies that things may not be where you would like them to be at present; however, there is a belief that with communication and understanding, by the close of the letter, things can be turned in a more favorable direction. A benediction is a pronouncement of a divine blessing given in the Bible; it represents a joyful and a unifying call to faith, patience, and practice for the faithful. Based on the certainty and divine principles of God, one of the most powerful things about gathering or adjoining yourself with a body of believers is the opportunity to speak life into situations where oftentimes there is only detriment. This is the time when the people of God assemble themselves together or when the people of God have the occasion to come face-to-face one with the other. This is a divine opportunity to speak life in some time what amounts to be very gloomy and hopeless situations. Oftentimes, we fail to understand the level of empowerment that God has given us through and by his Son, Jesus Christ, to speak those things that are not as though they were. The posture that is taken when your prayer published to God is not what prompts a move from him. Being on your knees or being on the altar are not prerequisites for speaking a blessing or a special anointing into someone's life and prompting a move of God. We, as the people of God, have failed in some regard to come to a full understanding of the revelation that is reserved in the scripture that says greater is he that already lives in us than he that is in the world. We spend more time and effort exploring what is wrong and chit-chatting about how bad it is than we do speaking the power that God has inevitably given us to overcome the power of the enemy. A benediction is typically a short, concise statement given in the

Bible in the form of a petition. An assurance, a promise, or even an established principle. It voices images of protection or comfort, an abundance, or some other word of assurance. Benediction simply means to say good or to voice good thoughts. To take this line of thought even further is to understand that what makes good thoughts good is that they are based on truth; they are based on principles. Whatever is true fulfils itself for it is based in God. Good is the inevitable result of the certainty and righteousness of the truth of God, who is all good, as the Bible tells us.

So as we begin to take a closer look and understand the ability that God has given us through and by faith, we coupled that with the spoken word to turn the tide of whatever may be evident in the atmosphere, wherever we find ourselves, at any given time. We find that we are also examining "principles," those things that have been logged and laid down by the eventuality of occurrences as dictated by the Word of God. Principles serve to unlock the mysteries that God has had hidden in his Word (Hebrews 11:6) to come to the aid of his people when they find themselves in maladjusted situations. The principles of God are built upon the foundations laid by the building blocks that serve as the laws of the Spirit that govern the manifestations to the flesh from the Spirit realm.

So we look at Proverbs 18:21, "Death and life are in the power of the tongue: and they that love it shall eat the fruit thereof."

We find that the tongue is a powerful tool that God has given you, and with the tongue, either the things that promote life will breathe and bring forth the blessings of God, or you will work to establish the detriment that the enemy is trying and working so diligently to make evident in your life. There are times when we desire to say good things but find ourselves at odds as to what we should say. This absence of prophetic utterance is an example of why it is so important that we make ourselves students of the Word of God, that we might live and walk in his principles and be governed by the power that is found therein, led by our relationship with him and our familiarity of his Word. We also read that the heart guides the tongue, and what is in you will govern what you eventually will say. We find in Proverbs 23:7, "For as he thinketh in his heart, so is he: Eat and drink, saith he to thee; but his heart is not with thee."

So our conversation in this chapter is one of coming against the devil with the words that God has given us, even in those times when you may not know that you are in the fight of your life. The Word of God is the antidote to whatever and wherever we find ourselves in our lives. You will find in your walk with the Lord that when you learn and practice these power scriptures over your life and the lives that you are connected with, along with practicing the principles of God, that oftentimes without even being fully aware and without really asserting much energy, you are actually wrestling with the enemy over what God said was yours. When you purpose to use salutations and benedictions in your audibilizing Spirit-led unctions that you have, in essence, rolled up your sleeves and you are actually wrestling with the devil. Through your understanding of the scriptures and the power they represent, you are punching in their noses demons that are engaged in areas of your life that you had no idea they were involved with.

Who are we? And how should we think about ourselves? How powerful will we be when we get the answers to those questions? Let's look at some power scriptures. "The Lord shall preserve thee from all evil: he shall preserve thy soul. The Lord shall preserve thy going out and thy coming in from this time forth, and even for evermore" (Psalms 121:7).

This scripture reflects that when you are facing trouble, one of the most powerful things that you can do for yourself or that anyone can do for you is to read this scripture. It is a principle of God that is founded on the law of God that says he cannot lie. Once someone who is anointed by the Spirit of God and led by the hand of God stands in your presence and speaks this type of word over your life, whatever demons are hard at work in your life at that particular time must begin the process of mapping out their evacuation from the things concerning you. This plan of escape by the enemy is prompted by the powerful word spoken and RECEIVED in the midst of the time in which you find yourself. This Word says that every evil work (doesn't matter altogether what it is) that is in operation in your life at that given time must cease its operation. It is impossible for this word to return back unto the Lord void of accomplishing that which it was sent forth to accomplish. There are countless opportunities to speak "strong words" over the lives of people as you come in contact with them.

"Now the God of hope fill you with all joy and peace in believing, that ye may abound in hope, through the power of the Holy Ghost" (Romans 15:13).

This scripture speaks while you are yet sitting gripped by the claws of sadness and rejection, not necessarily knowing which way to turn. Here comes a salutation. Here comes a benediction that speaks hope in the midst of the bowels of despair. This verse speaks no matter what you are going through, no matter how long you have been going through it. Because of the Holy Spirit prevailing in your life, he shall overcome the negativism that the enemy and his host have activated in your midst. And you are not even fully aware that, that word has taken root in your life, but because of the power that is found in the principles of God that are released by the mentioning of the Word of God by his Spirit, you and those around you will begin to be freed up from the demonic persuasion of the enemy, all because you made your mind up that aimless salutations such as "good-bye" does not work to the edification of mind, body, and spirit, but instead, "the Lord will give strength unto his people; the Lord will bless his people with peace" (Psalms 29:11). Understand that with this, you are speaking definitely.

You are speaking healing and wellness, oftentimes in areas that you are not even aware exist. It is important to understand that it is not as detrimental for the people of God to know what is wrong as it is for them to know what is right; you are less effective in the things of God in terms of bringing forth deliverance when you totally focus on what is wrong. Most anybody can sift around and discern what is wrong, but the power is in being able to ascertain what is right in the midst of what is wrong. You are of no consequence in terms of provoking a move of God in your life or in the life of someone else if all your faith will afford you to do is sit down and ponder on what is wrong. But the true move of God can be uncovered in the prose or the spaces between the words on the page in the Word of God from these power scriptures. The power that is very well capable of tearing down the walls of the enemy, because sitting around discussing what is wrong is not going to birth deliverance.

> Now God himself and our Father, and our Lord Jesus Christ, direct our way unto you. And the Lord make you to increase and abound in love one toward another, and toward all men, even as we do toward you: To the end he may stablish your hearts unblameable in holiness before God, even our Father, at the coming of our Lord Jesus Christ with all his saints. (1 Thessalonians 3:11–13)

See, as we train our minds and tongues to think and speak in this fashion, stuff begins to break, and you may not necessarily understand it was there nor that it has broken. When you begin to present faith in such a verbose manner, things begin to turn around that you had no idea where the pillars that supported the demonic forces that bound you. When you cause your focus, by faith, to be turned away from the obvious problem and allow your faith to lead you to the rock from whom all blessings flow, in whom is no variableness or shadow of turning, you begin to see the hidden mysteries, which are hidden in the principles of

God, take root in your life, and things begin to turn around from the obvious to the hopeful. It is not the obvious that you want in your life. It is those things that you are hoping for to replace what is evident and what is obvious. The types of friends that you need are not the ones who walk up and point out the obvious, but you need people in your life who will reinforce the blessings of God that have been spoken to you in your spirit and now reside in your mind and say, "Don't you worry. Things are going to get better. Don't you worry. Your blessings are on the move." You need somebody to speak a word in your life like, Psalms 89:52, "Blessed be the Lord for evermore. Amen, and Amen," or Jude 1:24–25, "Now unto him that is able to keep you from falling, and to present you faultless before the presence of his glory with exceeding joy, to the only wise God our Savior, be glory and majesty, dominion and power, both now and ever. Amen."

These scriptures will work for you while you are going through and while you are suffering with the unfolding events of your life. Even while seemingly you are living your very own reality show, you actually may have your very own horror movie playing out. However, do know your strength to escape your present reality is found in the Holy Scriptures that read, "Now the God of peace, that brought again from the dead our Lord Jesus, that great shepherd of the sheep, through the blood of the everlasting covenant, make you perfect in every good work to do his will, working in you that which is well pleasing in his sight, through Jesus Christ; to whom be glory for ever and ever. Amen" (Hebrews 12:20).

Now that is a word spoken over your life that's powerful enough to cover whatever the matter might be. It says may the grace of God live bountifully in your life and the peace of God cover you from the crown of your head to the soles of your feet. A good stern handshake accompanied by a cliché-type remark with no thought of provoking a move of God in the life of the person being greeted does not compare to a handshake given with an eye-to-eye glare and words that say, "May God bless you, and may heaven smile upon you. I pray that God carries you and take you to wherever he has purposed for your life." Sometimes, we go through so much, and even through our best efforts, pride abounds to the point where we get self-conscious even when a prophetic word of God's grace is given with no prior warning. We question the purpose of the word and feel it necessary to discount the need for the word based on our understanding of where we are in life. We may find ourselves saying, "I am okay," or "There is nothing wrong with me," but the fact of the matter is, the word of consolation and exhortation did not say that anything was wrong, but it did imply that in the name of Jesus everything is now made right. Through the power of the tongue by faith, God has given us dominion over the times of our lives.

Learn to lean on your brothers and sisters and how to put power on your salutations, and the testimonies of God's goodness and grace will follow you no matter where you go. Speak a "good word" over yourself and those you come in contact with. Speak a word that prompts a move of God, one that causes the anointing of God to take root in the life of the receiver. Remember that deliverance does not need the agreement of the delivered to work. When the right hand is shook and the right faith is prompted, guided by the right understanding, deliverance will come.

> Grace be with all them that love our Lord Jesus Christ in sincerity. Amen. (Ephesians 6:24)

> The grace of the Lord Jesus Christ, and the love of God, and the communion of the Holy Ghost, be with you all. Amen. (1 Corinthians 13:14)

> And God is able to make all grace abound toward you; that ye, always having all sufficiency in

all things, may abound to every good work. (2 Corinthians 9:8)

> The Lord bless thee, and keep thee: The Lord make his face shine upon thee, and be gracious unto thee: The Lord lift up his countenance upon thee, and give thee peace. (Numbers 6:24–26)

Can you imagine your reaction if you actually were greeted in this fashion on a continual basis.

> And be not conformed to this world: but be ye transformed by the renewing of your mind, that ye may prove what is that good, and acceptable, and perfect, will of God. (Romans 12:2)

> Finally, brethren, farewell. Be perfect, be of good comfort, be of one mind, live in peace; and the God of love and peace shall be with you. (2 Corinthians 13:11)

> But ye, beloved, building up yourselves on your most holy faith, praying in the Holy Ghost. Keep yourselves in the love of God, looking for the mercy of our Lord Jesus Christ unto eternal life. (Jude 1:20–21)

> There be many that say, "Who will shew us any good? Lord, lift thou up the light of thy countenance upon us." (Psalms 4:6)

Certainly, I could go on and on. The point is that it is important that you speak a good strong word over yourself and those who you love and are acquainted with. Do not allow the enemy to cause you to underestimate the anointing that you have, the positive outlook that you have, in the worst of times believing that you serve the only true and living God. Take your time and speak a "good word," a fresh strong word, born not of the flesh but of the Spirit spawned by faith. After you spend time speaking life on others, do not forget to speak life over yourself. When things are falling down all around you and no immediate help is apparent anywhere you look and when it seems like no one really understands your plight or cares, when someone comes upon you and asks you how you are doing, tell them, "I am blessed," "I am anointed," and "I am highly favored." It might not be evident right then, but speak that word over your own self. That you are blessed and you know you are blessed. You are anointed, and you know you are anointed. You are highly favored, and you know you are highly favored to do the will and fulfill the purpose of God in your life.

It is not good to speak the obvious for the enemy operates in this realm, and most of what we see and experience in this realm is the byproduct of the hand of Satan. Be mindful that you cannot necessarily see with the natural eye what God is doing. You can't see it but refuse to let that stop you from believing it. Him that God has called, he is able to keep from falling and to present faultless before the presence of his glory with exceeding joy. If God said it, he is going to do it. Negative talk is of little to no consequence when you go back and look at your testimony.

When you look at blessed, anointed, and highly favored and consider them one at a time, you can see the total picture. Let's look at blessed. You have got to look at your life and come to a place where you recognize and understand and agree with the notion that since you were a child, the hand and anointing of God has been over your life, and what money could not do, God did it! What folks could not do, God did it! From the day God brought you into this world, you have been blessed. When it looked like things were not going to work out, God blessed you. When you got sick, even as children, even as babies, God kept you. When parents did not have the resources to it get it done, God stepped in and did it. If you can't say anointed or highly favored, you can say, "blessed." Let's look at anointed. Can you testify that there has been something different about you your entire life? Maybe you have not approached or seen things quite in the way that other people do. The anointing of God sets one aside from the rest. It works to order the steps of the designated in such a way that the purpose of God in the life of the called unfolds in the midst of the contradiction that is that person. The hand of God is on your life; there is some facet of ministry that you were born to attend to. You may not be comfortable with it, but there is some facet of ministry that you were born to attend to.

Let's talk about highly favored. When you are blessed, when you are anointed, God opens the door, and he makes the ways to put you in position where the blessings and the anointing of your life might be of consequence in the lives of other people. Be certain to understand that you did not choose where you are but the hand of God systematically placed you where you are. Be it that you are fanatical or not, the hand of God is on your life, and the times of your life are in his hands. You are not going to fall or fail because the hand of God is holding you up in the midst of it all. Scream out in your spirit right now, and declare that you are blessed. Regardless of what the enemy may want you to see, proclaim that you are blessed and that you are anointed and that you are highly favored.

Sometimes in the fourth watch of the night, it will come down to the dead time. It will come to now or never, but things will open up right on time. Consider Joseph of biblical times (Genesis 37:18-36), and how he was sold into slavery because he was blessed and because he was different. There was a different kind of anointing on Joseph, and his brothers could not appreciate it. Every now and then, you will run into people who will not and cannot appreciate the diversity God has placed in your life because of the anointing. Be it having to deal with people who cannot appreciate the way you love or people who cannot appreciate the way you give of yourself. The anointed of God know what it means to be different and to stick out. Joseph stuck out like a sore thumb. When he tried not to stick out, he'd stick out. It is impossible to hide the anointing of God for long. The anointing will show. It will leak out and make itself evident.

The brothers of Joseph grew to hate him because of the nature of his anointing and his willingness to share freely the evidence of it. Joseph was so free-hearted and had such an open, innocent spirit that every time God would show him something, he would run and tell it. It is important to understand that your happiness does not always translate to the happiness of those around you.

The favor that was on his life prompted his father, Isaac, to make him a coat of many colors. This complicated stuff even more, simply because the coat had colors in it that individually were the colors of his brothers. The gift of God in you will make room for you, and those who have God will give more, and the hatred of his brothers for him intensified because they recognized that in him was every one of them. Remember, the evil heart does not like to see you excel in areas that they reserved for themselves but failed to aspire to. Eventually, they planned to get rid of him. They planned to kill him off. Even though they plotted against him, the hand of God was on his life. Their plotting against him was a part of God's master plan. The revelation is that it took the plotting of the enemy to get you where God intended for you to be. If someone had not lied on you, you would have never gotten to where you were supposed to be. The work God had for you cannot be done at home or in your familiar place. You will have to be driven to the place of your purpose destined by the hand of God. Joseph was sold into slavery, but that was a blessing for the intent was to kill him. No weapon formed against you will prosper; you think what happened manifested and was made evident was bad, but if you only knew what the devil wanted to do, you would lose yourself in praise this very moment. Joseph was blessed, and when they threw him in the pit and sold him into slavery and he ended up in Potiphar's house and rose up to prominence in the house of his slave master, he was highly favored. See, favor says that no matter where you find yourself at some point, you are going to rise to the top. You may start off at the bottom, but before long, the favor of God will see to your promotion and ascension to the top. Speak it over your own life. "I have the favor of God. I have the favor of God." The people of God must go back and grab faith and understand that anointing on your life and recognize that all you need to do as a child of God is just get your "foot in the door." Pay no mind and lose sight of what you have lost overtime because that's in the past, and it has driven you to where you are presently. You must learn to rejoice when God allows you to just get your "foot in the door." By faith, you must believe the anointing of God on your life so much so you say, "If I can just get my foot in the door, this anointing and the favor of God on my life will do the rest." Satan will tell you that you are too close to the bottom and that your time for where you are has long past and you should be further along by now. But by the power of God invested in you, you tell that devil, "I am blessed, I am anointed, and I am highly favored, and this anointing on my life told me that I am destined for greatness, and wherever my feet shall trod, my God has given to me as a possession.

So we find that everywhere that Joseph found himself and got his foot in the door, it was just a matter of time before he went from the "gutter-most" to the uttermost. Because it was unmistakable and undeniable and irrefutable that he was blessed, anointed, and highly favored.

# The Next Best Thing

And Moses said unto the Lord, "See, thou sayest unto me, 'Bring up this people:' and thou hast not let me know whom thou wilt send with me. Yet thou hast said, 'I know thee by name, and thou hast also found grace in my sight.' Now therefore, I pray thee, if I have found grace in thy sight, shew me now thy way, that I may know thee, that I may find grace in thy sight: and consider that this nation is thy people." And he said, "My presence shall go with thee, and I will give thee rest." And he said unto him, "If thy presence go not with me, carry us not up hence. For wherein shall it be known here that I and thy people have found grace in thy sight? Is it not in that thou goest with us? So shall we be separated, I and thy people, from all the people that are upon the face of the earth." And the Lord said unto Moses, "I will do this thing also that thou hast spoken: for thou hast found grace in my sight, and I know thee by name." And he said, "I beseech thee, shew me thy glory." And he said, "I will make all my goodness pass before thee, and I will proclaim the name of the Lord before thee; and will be gracious to whom I will be gracious, and will shew mercy on whom I will shew mercy." And he said, "Thou canst not see my face: for there shall no man see me, and live."

And the Lord said, "Behold, there is a place by me, and thou shalt stand upon a rock: And it shall come to pass, while my glory passeth by, that I will put thee in a clift of the rock, and will cover thee with my hand while I pass by: And I will take away mine hand, and thou shalt see my back parts: but my face shall not be seen." (Exodus 33:12–22)

We are coming out with our hands up! Coming out with my praise intact. Greatness is on the way, and even now, God is doing something spectacular, and whether you know it or not, "It is good for us to be here." As we look at this text and draw some understanding as to what has occurred, as we began to examine the word of God for a clearer understanding as to what has happened in the word and how the happening applies to us today, our minds must go back and recall that prior to this chapter, something very treacherous has happened in the midst of the children of Israel. We find that God has brought Moses a long way since the days of the burning bush, which sat on the mountainside and burned and could not be consumed. It is clear that God has brought Moses a long way from the point of inception, where God told him, "I am going to send you to be a savior of sorts for my people Israel." By this point of the scriptures, time has already transpired and the ten plagues have already run their course and Pharaoh has already been softened by the hand of God to the point where he had released the people of God under their own recognizance. By the time we catch up with Moses here in the thirty-third chapter of Exodus, Moses is on Mt. Sinai waiting for God's instruction. God has already, with the finger of his own hand, reached into granite rock and carved out the words on tablets of stone that would serve as the Ten Commandments for his people. With these tablets, Moses was instructed to return to his people, however somewhere between getting the word and delivering the word to the children of Israel, a strange noise rose up out of the camp. Isn't it something how we can get all excited about what God has called us to do, but when we look around, we find that a lot of folks who are with us are not necessarily with us. It is possible to be occupying the same space but not be in the same place. This is Moses's predicament at this particular time because Moses began to be incited by the Lord as God began to transfer ownership for the children of Israel over to him. God began to tell him that, "*Thy* people that *you* brought up out of Egypt are a stiff-necked people and have corrupted themselves." Can you imagine being Moses at this particular time? Understand that before God called Moses, he never aspired to be a deliverer. He was comfortably found tending the flocks of his father-in-law, and as far as he knew, his days were to be spent doing just that. But it was God who ordained Moses to lead his people; however, as soon as the people of God began to behave in a manner contrary to the way a chosen people of God should, God termed them as Moses's people. God went as far as to say, "These people are your people that you brought up out of Egypt. They are some hard-headed and stiff-necked people." In the midst of writing the tablets, God halted Moses and told him that he needed to get off the mountain while his anger was kindled to a point of action against this stiff-necked people.

God made it clear that his intentions were to kill the nation right at the base of the mountain. This is where Moses showed his worthiness and the excellence of choice that God had made in choosing him as leader of the nation. Moses spoke up and defended the children of Israel against the wrath of God and helped to quench God's rush to judgment against his children. Moses stood in the gap for the people. He said, "God, you cannot kill them for if you kill them, the surrounding nations will declare that you brought them out of Egypt no more than to slay them." And Moses stood there and talked with and reasoned with God.

God said, "I hear you. Now go on down." When Moses finally got down to where the people were, he recognized that the people were all out of sorts. He also recognized that his brother Aaron had led the people astray by collecting their gold. He took their earrings, he took their necklaces, he took their rings, he took many of the artifacts that they had been blessed by the Egyptians upon their departure from Egypt, and he used those artifacts to erect something in a new place that served to remind them of the old places.

It is important that we feel Moses's pain right now because this letdown did not come at the hand of someone he did not know, but it came at the hand of his brother, someone he trusted with his anointing and life. This place is the place where pain changes relationships forever. This is the place where reality introduces himself to the unexpecting child of God. The place where naivety is replaced by growth and wisdom in the things of God. So we find that when this occurred to Moses, really what had transpired was he questioned Aaron and asked him, "What have these people done to you for you to cause them to sin against God?" See, in essence, the respect that Moses had given Aaron in the view of the people is what had actually put Aaron in a position with the people where they trusted him to lead them in Moses's absence. Remember, people will infer trustworthiness by what they perceive the level of acceptance is of that individual by their leadership. The question that Moses asked Aaron may be of no consequence to some, but many of us understand what it feels like to have your feelings hurt, and we understand full well what it means to be betrayed. We understand what it is like to reach back for help just to find that no true help really exist at that given time. I believe that, at this particular time, Moses's heart was bleeding as he looked at Aaron, his brother, and thought if it had not been for him, they would not be suffering this setback.

I also feel Moses's pain as he also grapples with the notion that after all this, God has transferred ownership of and for the people over to him. In his heart, Moses had come to a place of halt, where by his involvement with the mission of God was more than he could mentally facilitate. Moses, in his dissecting of the unfolding effects, was left with a truth that dictated to him that these people indeed where not his but they belonged to God. Right, wrong, or indifferent, these were God's people. It is important that anyone designated to lead anything for God be mindful of this very fact. The people you lead, no matter how imperfect, belong to a perfect God, and they are his and his alone. Know who you are and where your people responsibility stops and your God responsibility starts if you have ever been called to anything that looks like ministry. You need to understand that no matter how much you love the people or how much you care about the people, they are not your people; they belong to God.

As long as you walk around as though the ministry and the responsibility for the people belongs to you, you will continually have a heavy heart and a broken spirit. Finally, we find Moses here in our text scripture coming to the realization that the only business he has with the Lord's people is God's business and that since it is God's business, any issues concerning the Business is better served when presented to God in Prayer. This is where we find Moses in our text scripture.

Moses is going back to God and saying, "Excuse me, Mr. God, but you remember in the thirty-second chapter, where you said that these hard-headed folks were my folks? I don't mean to contradict you, but these are your folks, and these are your people. Furthermore, you told me to come bring them out of Egypt, and it just occurred to me that out of all of this walking we have done, you have not told us where we are going." I wonder if you were to be honest, if you would say that you have been working for Jesus, and it is dawning on you now that out of all of your doing, he has not altogether told you where you are going.

The nature of prayer is once you get started, it is like water that has been let lose. Once you get started making your petitions known to God, you begin to tell God everything. And Moses said, "By the way, not only do we not know where we are going, but I need to know you better than I know you." The truth of the matter is that when God first calls his chosen, it sounds to the called as if what he is calling them to do is something they can actually get done. Until they start the process of dealing with what must be dealt with to bring the task from inception to completion, through to victory, that's when they throw up their hands and say, "God, I have got to get to know you better. I didn't know that people were going to behave like this. I did not know that things were going to turn out like this. I didn't know my best friend was going to walk off and leave me. I didn't know that I was going to be lied on, rebuked, and scorned, just for trying to serve you." And Moses said, "I have got to get to know you better." Moses said three things profoundly, "These are your people. I don't know where I am going, and now I know if I am going to make it, I have got to get to know you better."

Knowing God better is a powerful revelation from Moses straight to us, because as you revisit the story of the delivering of the children of Israel from Egyptian rule, you find that God had already used Moses mightily. How is it that you could be used by God to transform a rod into a serpent, or how is it that God can use you to turn water into blood or hail to fire and there be a need for more intimacy with God? How is it that you can speak a word and flies cover the earth, yet aspects of your relationship with God that will enable you to complete your mission in him not be fully intact? The answer to those questions are found in the realization that as you begin to go forth in obedience and walk in the gift that God has called you to walk in—be it prophecy, evangelism, pastoral, apostleship, or the gifts of administration—it is not long before you find out that you cannot make it on the gift alone.

The prophet has to find out that prophesy is not enough to take him through alone. The tongue speaker has got to find out that speaking in tongues is not enough to take him through alone. Therefore, when Moses came to the realization that this relationship conversation was crucial to his survival, he took the rod, the gift of God, the instrument of miracles given to him to aide him in achieving his ultimate purpose in God, and he leaned it up in a corner somewhere. When a relationship with God is what is required to achieve your purpose in him, you must learn to take the gift of God that is in you and lean it up in a corner somewhere. Sometimes, you need God to take you to another level, and you have to take your gift and say, "God, this is not about the gift now. This is about relationship. I have got to get to know you better for myself, beyond the gift and beyond the call on my life. It is crucial for me and detrimental to my faith that I get to see you in a very real and practical way that strikes to the core of who I am and reinforces your [God's] involvement in the very real struggles involved with achieving my ultimate destination in you."

This time, Moses took the rod and laid it in the corner. There are times when being a big-time prophet, preacher, teacher is not good enough simply because prophets, preachers, and teachers have bills too. Preachers have problems in their homes too. And every now and then, you have got to take your gift and stand it in the corner and pull on God with a request that says, "God Relationship."

"Take me back to when you first called me. God, take me back to the place where nobody knew my name. God, take me back to the place I was before I found out even who I am in you. Take me back, God, to that place where you touched me and told me if I go, you would go with me. Take me to the place, God, where you told me if I open my mouth, you would speak for me. Take me to the place, God, where you told me you would never leave me nor forsake me."

Sometimes, people will look at you, and they only see the glory, and they only hear the applause. They only see the people facing you, and they may somehow formulate the audacity to be jealous of who they think you are and what they think you have, but if they could be you for one day, they would *wreck your life*. When you are anointed of God, if you were to hand your haters control of your life for one day, they would drive your life into the ditch simply because they would not be able to handle your life and the complexities of God that it takes to keep it in order. They could not handle being you. If your haters knew what it took to be you, they would not waste their time being jealous. If they knew what it took to be you, they would not waste their time hating on you. If they knew what it takes to be you instead of trying to stop, hinder, and block you, they would try to help you. God is holding you together! People need not let the evidence of the hand of God in your life fool them! God is holding you together! What people don't understand is, if God was not holding you together, you would totally lose your mind. "If God were not holding you together, you would most certainly go to pieces. If God were not holding you together, you would be the biggest fool in the world. If God were not holding you together, you would not have him on your mind.

So the reoccurring theme behind Moses's request is the fact that he did not know what he was getting into when he accepted the call. This realization is one that is common to the called people of God, who have been tasked with a godly duty in him. This notion surfaces when we compare the imagined particulars of our call, which are formed by our mental projection of our understanding of probability with the reality of where we find ourselves when we become self-aware in the midst of our God mission. Case in point, from the outset, Moses knew that there was great potential for complication involved with what he was being called to do because Moses's past experiences dictated to him, and he knew how the Egyptian government worked, and he knew that the Egyptians were dependent on the Israelites. So from inception, he knew that it was a tough task; however, even with what he thought he knew, he did not know how tough of a job he was actually getting into because common sense dictates that slaves don't want to be slaves. Yes, it was understood by Moses that it was a rough job, but at the end of the day, one would think that if the task is to liberate the people from hardship to a land that flowed with milk and honey, common sense says that the people would not only want to go but patiently endure the hardships of transition until the day of realizing the promise. But what we find on this walk is that common sense has little to nothing to do with the reality of being called of God to accomplish something great in him. Such is the case today when witnessing to drug addicts that Jesus saves and then find that you practically have to chase them down in the streets just to get them in the house of the Lord. That is proof positive that "common sense" does not vote well in this line of work. And when you got saved and found out that this walk with God was real good and that it was better than the honey in the honeycomb, common sense told you that everybody you know wanted to feel like you felt, but it did not take long for you to find out that "common sense" has little to nothing to do with "God sense." And if you were to be completely honest, you did not know what you were getting yourself into when you accepted the call of God on your life. You didn't know that you would lose some of your closest friends as a result of your relationship with God. Some have found that sweethearts have turned their backs on them and treated them less than hospitable when they got serious about the call of God on their lives. No, we really had no idea what we were getting into at the time of the acceptance of the call of God on our lives. All we really knew at the time is that we felt something provoking us from the inside out. All we knew is that God touched us, we obeyed the call, but we really did not know altogether what we were getting ourselves into.

Moses did not know, and it took time for him to find out that he needed something more than a rod and a mouthpiece. Moses explicitly indicated that he needed to see God's face. Moses said, "I need to see you!" See the burning bush experience; it was good, but re-enforcement was now in order. The same goes for our testimony. It is good enough for a season. Certainly, it has been enough to bring you from where you were to where you are. But NOW, the cry is, "God, I need you to do something else. NOW, I am going to need more if I am going to be able to achieve in you by you." The bush burning and not being consumed was enough to get Moses to Egypt, but he knew that if he was going to make it to Canaan, he was going to need to see something else NOW. He needed God to share more concerning himself to establish a deeper and broader base for relationship with him. He, in essence, needed God to increase him in his knowledge of him and thereby equip him for the task at hand. Moses's cry basically proclaimed that if he were to be able to make it to his purpose, he needed God to share more of himself. There comes a time when all of us must approach God in all humility and make it known to him that WE NEED SOME MORE, WE NEED SOME MORE, AND WE NEED SOME MORE. Before this point, every time Moses thought about quitting, he saw in the memory of his mind, stimulated by the necessity of his faith, the bush burning yet not consumed. With this, Moses also would recall the hand that was placed in his bosom and came out white with leprosy, went back in, and came out clean. But NOW, Moses is saying, "God, you are taking me somewhere that is on an entirely different level. God, you are taking me somewhere now that is in another, space, time, and hemisphere, and I need a move of you that substantiates where you are taking me." That is an awesome request that you should make of the Lord even now. "LORD, I NEED A MOVE OF YOU NOW THAT SUBSTANTIATES WHERE YOU ARE TAKING ME! If you are taking me deeper in the Spirit, God, I need a Spirit move now. I need to see some mysteries. I need to see some doors open that only you can open. I need to see some ways being made that only you can make. If you are taking me deeper, GO ON AND TAKE ME THEN! Take me deeper if you are taking me deeper."

So we hear Moses, and he is partitioning God, saying, "I need to see your face. I need to see you, God." Can't you feel Moses praying the same prayer as you saying, "I need to see you. I got to see you, God. I heard you speaking to me, but now I need to see you. I felt you in my spirit, but now I need to see you. I was inclined to believe that you were in the midst of it, but NOW I need to see you."

Let's examine God's response to Moses's request. God said, "You cannot see me." Now think about that, what seemingly was such a simple request, being met by God with an out-and-out rejection to fulfill as requested. God's response indicated that Moses did not need to see him in the fashion that Moses was so thoroughly convinced that he needed to see him in. God elaborated on why Moses's request, though well-articulated, was not one founded in wisdom. God made it clear to Moses that if he was to be granted what he felt he needed in the form that he requested it, that the very thing he thought he needed would be too much for him and ultimately spell his demise. God told him that if he saw him physical to spiritual, he would die. Ultimately, his flesh could not handle the wholeness of God. The understanding is that faith has to be cultivated, like a culture in a petri dish. Ultimately, God takes us on the proper route to grow us by faith to the place in him that will ultimately enable us to complete our purpose in him. Seeing God in his totality defeats faith, and without faith, it is impossible to please God. Enoch progressively walked with God initially by faith, and that walk by faith eventually phased into knowing God in the fullness of who he is. At that very point of God awareness, Enoch became so taken with God and consumed by the knowledge of God's existence that he was no longer found with man but was taken by God. In essence, faith is the bridge between what is physically obtainable and what is spiritually founded. Once faith hardens, it becomes physical, and a natural manifestation is eminent. Enoch disappeared because his faith was realized; Enoch believed his way to God.

In the case of Moses and the rest of us, God made it clear that he could not see his face but he would share with him all he needed to achieve the essence of his request. God knew full well what Moses was getting at, and he also knew from what place in Moses his question was derived. God, in essence, told Moses that seeing his face was out of the question but he would share with him the "next best thing," HIS GLORY!

To see the glory of God is the next best thing to seeing God himself. We cannot look upon his face, but to see his Glory is to realize him, and to realize him is to come to a place within yourself that he is real and that he is in control and that he is more than capable of handling any issues that can fit in our hands. With the revealing of his glory, he is declaring that he is about to make a "praiser" out of you. He is about to make a worshipper out of you and that he is about to take you somewhere in faith and that he is getting ready to do the next best thing. When a man has faith, what does he need with seeing? When a man has hope, he has seen it already.

God said, "You cannot see me, but I tell you what I am going to do." He declared to Moses, "The reason you feel so unsettled and the reason your spirit is turned upside down is because you are on shaky ground. You are nervous and you do not know how things are going to turn out. You are staring failure in the face, and your faith is failing fast. The first thing I am going to do is I am going to pick you up and put you on a rock." In this, God steadied Moses's feet, and he steadied his steps; he established him on a rock. In the midst of the call on your life, at times you may feel shaky, and at times you may want to give up, but God is asking, "Where are you going? You are not excused, and you are not dismissed." Maybe you know someone who has declared that they have had enough and that they are throwing in the towel, that they are sick of the whole thing and they are about ready to let someone else carry the banner now. But before you let them walk away from their godly duty, echo the question of God in their hearing that repeats, "Where are you going? Because you are not excused, and you are not dismissed." God is saying, in the midst of it all, that he has not excused you to quit. You might walk off, but you are not excused. You might get missing, but you are not excused. That's why Jeremiah the prophet proclaimed that God is married to the backslider. God is saying, "Get back here." I know your feelings are hurt, I know your heart is broken, I know you are sick and tired, but God told me to tell you to get back here, because you are not excused.

The next best thing—no face, but all glory. So God placed Moses in the cliff of the rock, and as his glory passed by, the wind began to stir up in the same fashion that it stirred up in Isaiah 6, when the glory train filled the room. The noise of God's magnificence proceeded him. Exodus 34:5–8 proclaims,

> And the Lord descended in the cloud, and stood with him there, and proclaimed the name of the Lord. And the Lord passed by before him, and proclaimed, "The Lord, The Lord God, merciful and gracious, longsuffering, and abundant in goodness and truth. Keeping mercy for thousands, forgiving iniquity and transgression and sin, and that will by no means clear the guilty; visiting the iniquity of the fathers upon the children, and upon the children's children, unto the third and to the fourth generation. And Moses made haste, and bowed his head toward the earth, and worshipped.

Look at the similarities to what is written in Isaiah 6:3–4, "And one cried unto another, and said, Holy, holy, holy, is the Lord of hosts: the whole earth is full of his glory. And the posts of the door moved at the voice of him that cried, and the house was filled with smoke."

You cannot praise God like he should be praised, and it is impossible to worship God like he deserves to be worshipped with a heavy heart, tainted by glimpses of depression. It takes a thankful heart caught up in the throes of faith and bathed in a realization of his glory to give him a proper praise and a heartfelt worship. Somewhere along the line, a realization of who God is has got to enter into your mind and enter into your heart. Not a flirtatious praise or a light-hearted worship, but a life-changing breaking of the spirit that catapults you into a place in worship that was totally motivated by an increase in your faith in God. A drenching of the spirit that can only come through by a God encounter. A quickening that says, "God, if it had not been for you, who was on my side, where would I be?" A revelation that says, "God, you are God, and truly, I am your servant." So we see Moses here in the midst of God's glory being revealed coming to a place in himself where he recognizes that worship was in order. Mind you, prior to this revealing of the glory of God, Moses was standing in the presence of the Most High. It was only when he came face-to-face with God's glory that the gravity of who God is forced him to his knees. Isn't it something how we can stand in the presence of God and lose sight of just who he is and what he represents? Isn't it something how in the midst of our feeling sorry for ourselves and feeling like we cannot go on, our testimonies are delivered to us first-class mail by the Holy Spirit and we begin to remember where God has brought us from and where, as we were feeling bad, we begin to bow down and lower our heads in worship to him who is worthy of the praise. And Moses began to give God glory because of the glory. See, you give God glory because of his glory, and when you think of the goodness of Jesus and all that he has done for you, your soul cries out, "Hallelujah! I thank God for saving me!"

You can't see his face, but he gave you the next best thing, when he let you see his glory! When you begin to understand that nobody could do this but God, nobody could do this but the Lord, then you are seeing his glory. When you begin to understand that it wasn't anybody but Jesus who brought you all the way, you are seeing his glory. Maybe he did not pay all your outstanding bills, and maybe you did not get that new car or house that you anointed for weeks on end, but you still owe God the praise for his glory for his glory transcends our needs and speaks to who he is. In seeing God's glory, you will gain the strength needed to move closer to your designated end in him.

Many may look on your present positioning as it relates to your ultimate purpose and ascertain that you should be further along the path to perfection than you presently are. My advice to you is that you not worry about the input of your critics and always remember that they do not know the cost of your alabaster box. They have no idea the price you have had to pay to be where you are now. So thank God for where you are and where he has promised to take you. The truth of the matter is, you have not seen Jesus, and you have not seen God, but you have seen their glory. Every time you look in the mirror, you are looking at their glory. Every time you look in the mirror, you are looking at God's handy work. No matter what it looks like, something on the inside is saying, "Go ahead." You are here because God has great expectations for you. You are here because God intends to do something awesome in your life. He is already performing it, and he is performing it by his glory. Not by your pocketbook, but by his glory. Not by the name on the tags of your clothes, but by his glory. Not by the company you keep, but by his glory. Not by your paystub or the lack thereof, but by his glory. At the end of the day, we were rescued by God to work for God. Moses never saw God's face; however, he did see God's backside. God's backside represents the evidence of his involvement. Oftentimes, we cannot denote when God showed up, but we can certainly tell that he has been there. The evidence of a move of God is his glory in the making. I wonder if you have ever caught a glimpse of God on his way out. Maybe God came in and delivered you from an addiction. You can't quite put your finger on when; however, the evidence is there in your deliverance that he had been there. And now, when people that you used to frequent come in contact with you, they have a hard time believing that you are the same person, but because of the youthfulness of the glory of God, they find it difficult to believe that you are the same person.

Thank God for allowing you to see his glory. Testify to the fact that you have seen his glory, and only a loving kind, gracious, merciful God could do for you what has been done. Confess to him that you give him the glory for his glory. You give him the praise for his glory. You magnify his name for his glory. You promote him to where he is and to where he should be in you. Cause your mind to be elevated to the places where God abounds. Demand your mind to get up to the high places laden with hope where God resides. Understand that God is not going to descend to the base of the mountain to meet with us. We must be prepared to ascend to the high places where he resides. Climb up on the mountain where you can have him all to yourself. Where you can make your petitions known with no shame, understanding that he can see past your covering to your shame. There is no need to hide shame because there is no covering that hides us from God. We never need to hide our feelings because he can see our feelings. We may as well share our feelings with God in an act of worship. Practice relationship-building exercises with God in the form of worship. Tell him, "God I need you now." Tell him, "I don't always feel the way I should be feeling, and I don't always look the way I should look, but I need you now."

This is your life, and God's glory is going to help you get through it. We don't get to trade it in. Moses wanted to trade it in, but the truth of the matter is Moses did not have a home. The hand of God kept Moses. Moses had escaped from Egypt twice—once on his way to find his God and once as the deliverer for his God. If Moses were to draw back on God now, where would he go? In essence, he is homeless. He was a stowaway from a child. The revelation here is that we all have been set up to serve God. You, Moses, and I have been set up to do something great in God. The enemy may tell us that we have somewhere to go, but contrary to popular belief, God rescued us from where we were. We owe God! Where are you going? You are where you are going! We are where we are by the grace of God. Just as Moses before us, we are where we were born to be. We are in the midst of our purpose being driven by our destiny and motivated by our faith. And there is nothing else for us to do now but get better. All we can do now is get more proficient. All we can do now is get more prophetic. All we can do now is get more serious and committed. There is nowhere for you to go. Get it together in the name of Jesus! The hand of God is all over you. I dare you to raise your hands right now and start thinking about who you are and who he is and go into a place of worship in your heart, and then let what is in your heart flow from your lips and begin to defy the forces of the enemy by thanking God. Give God glory; give him praise! Ask him to bid you to come up to him. Let me come up! Make it known, Father, that I have a need to come up. Make it known that staying where you are and dying in your faith and mind is not an option. Make it known that being in church and amongst the saints and dying spiritually is not an option. Maybe your praise and worship has been lacking, but if he helps you come up, you can get up. Satan has got to leave you alone when he says, "Come up." Demons and demonic forces have got to release your mind when he says, "Come up." For seeing his glory is the Next Best Thing to seeing his face.

# Fight The Devil On His Terms

"(For the weapons of our warfare are not carnal, but mighty through God to the pulling down of strong holds;) Casting down imaginations, and every high thing that exalteth itself against the knowledge of God, and bringing into captivity every thought to the obedience of Christ" (2 Corinthians 2:4).

These very compact verses found in the writings of Paul so graciously enlightens us to the fact that our weapons of choice as we war against the enemy cannot be of this world. This understanding speaks to our potential and how often we are met with different types of situations and distresses or when we are met with issues and problems. We are drawn into a place in our minds by the enemy where we envision that what we are dealing with is something that we can handle in our flesh. If we are not careful, we begin the process of fighting based on our instruments of detection and perception. We begin to present ourselves in our warfare or in our resistance to the enemy by utilizing the tools within ourselves that served to alert us to instance of the upheaval initially. We employ our eyes, and with them, we speculate as to what we think is happening. We use our ears, and we hear what is being said concerning the situation. We begin the process of just not feeling right; our senses tell us that something concerning the times is out of kilter, and therefore because these senses are derived from our carnal flesh, the warfare that we began to embark upon against the enemy is not one against the enemy but one against the knowledge of the situation or the carnal presentation by the enemy. We begin to fight the evidence of what he is doing, never touching the culprit of what is being done. "A never-ending cycle." Simply because our sensory devices that cause us to be alerted to fact that a problem is at hand are oftentimes born of the flesh, when we begin to think about antidotes to the issues at hand, they too are born of the flesh. We try to deflate what we see and feel by what we do. We try to compensate for what we hear by what we say. In essence, our defense to what is presented to us is no more than something else that is born in our flesh that we deem a proper counter to what we are perceiving.

So if we are not walking in the Spirit, when we recognize the need for money, we begin to seek natural means to alleviate the problem. As we become sensitive to different things in the flesh, we begin to ponder what we can do. So indeed, it is in these times that our text scripture very well may be the very last thing that we think about. We very well do not come into the knowledge of what we are going through or that what we are dealing with is not carnal. We do not ascertain that if we meet the issue at hand with combatants born of this world, that our time of trial is only going to be prolonged. This detaining of the move of God by his Spirit, in essence, is only going to cast us into a place where we find ourselves in the grasps of conflict longer than is necessary. Only if we understood fully that the weapons, or our methods of resolution, to combat what we are going through cannot be born of the flesh. But my faith must, first of all, educate me. My faith must alert me to the fact that what I am dealing with is not of the flesh. Sometimes, we go through things for long periods before we allow faith to have her perfect work. We go through for periods on end, sometimes testifying that we are believing God while we are yet saying we are believing God. We have a measure of trust in our own flesh to add dimensions of resolution to the issues at hand. Our lips rehearse that we believe God, while our flesh acts upon a call to dominance that says, "Let me go see what I can do." Our notion of who God is must dominate in our times of trouble. So the first essential to letting faith have her perfect work is coming to an understanding that "what I am going through or what I am yet dealing with is not natural."

See, you cannot war in the Spirit and you cannot fight in the Spirit if you have not come to a resolution in your mind that says, "What I am dealing with is not of the flesh." Because as long as you are led to believe that what you are dealing with is of the flesh, your method of fighting will be born of the flesh. There must be a call to faith in the midst of your storm. A call to stand where the believer approaches the inevitability that the enemy is involved in the undergirding of the issues at hand. The saying commonly used is, "Never bring a knife to a gun fight," and when you fail to recognize that no matter how subtle or no matter how minute, deceptive, or small, the thing is that you as a child of God are going through, it was not born of the flesh, and you cannot win trying to war in the flesh. Some might reply to this with a statement that says, "When I put my mind to it, I can get out of anything." Well, my response to that simply is, "You are not getting out of anything. You are only prolonging your engagement with the thing." A failure to involve God is a failure to be delivered. So oftentimes, what we think is fixed and what subsided for a moment is only lying dormant to "pop up" at some other inopportune time for it has not been defeated. So explicitly, the weapons of "our" warfare are not carnal, and it is important that we take a close look at "our" here for that O-U-R is talking about the true-born believer—those of us who are counting on and relying on God for our direction, our keeping, and our not-so-obvious deliverance. That O-U-R speaks to what we so desperately depend on and what we are trusting God for. It says our weapons of warfare are not found solely in your credit report, it is not found solely in your tax return, it is not found solely in who you know, but it is found in your understanding of what weapons are afforded to you in the Spirit. DID YOU KNOW THAT WE HAVE WEAPONS? I contend to the body of Christ that many of us have heard concerning the weapons, but many of us are not astute and are not learned as to what the weapons are or how to use them. Just because you can hold a weapon does not mean that you know how to use it. Hearing about the weapons is not enough, and if we were to get serious and really honest, we would have to admit that we have not really used the weapons. We oftentimes move under the pretenses of what we have been taught at the expense of the experiences of others and not really walking in the knowledge of the scripture in Proverbs 4:7, which declares that wisdom is the principal thing, but with all thou getting, get understanding. We oftentimes are armed with the wisdom of a cannon in the Spirit and lack the understanding of a .22-caliber pistol. We read materials and are made aware of principles that are equated with having an AK-47 strapped to our sides yet lacking the life experience or Holy Spirit bearing discernment to properly operate a "spitball" shooter in the Spirit. So carrying a weapon does not necessarily constitute knowing how to properly use the weapon. Many of us have heard about "fasting," but if we were to be honest, we do not fast by faith the way we should. Many of us have heard about the power of prayer, but if we were to be totally honest about it, many times, the Spirit of the Lord has shaken us out of our sleep, and we have failed to get up out of bed and go and resign ourselves to prayer. Look at John 10:10, "The thief cometh not, but for to steal, and to kill, and to destroy: I am come that they might have life, and that they might have it more abundantly."

In looking at this passage, the Spirit of the Lord ministered to me that the enemy cannot steal what you have never possessed. The enemy cannot take that which was never yours. He cannot displace what was never "in place." You may not have what God said was yours now, but it does not mean you will never have it or that it was never purposed in the Spirit. It simply means that the enemy displaced it. If we do not do what is necessary or if we do not arm ourselves with what is necessary in the Spirit, we will continue to be victimized by the enemy as he manipulates and diminishes what God said was ours. Ultimately, the devil desires to defile the thing that God has predicated as the next move toward your purpose in your life. The enemy wants to distort the move of God so much so in your life that the end result of his tampering renders the next step in your evolution in God as being useless to you. The Bible declares in Psalms 37:23 *that the steps of a good man are ordered by the Lord.* Steps here imply the progressive nature of how God pieces the purpose of our lives together and arranges divinely the order of things that constitute the manifestation of his promises in the lives of his people. Each step is essential in our eventual arrival to that predestined place in God. Although your destination has been predestined, it does not mean you will ever get there. Ask Moses.

Many of us from the pulpit to the door are living beneath our privilege simply because we fail to utilize the weapons. We sing about the weapons. We preach concerning the weapons. We talk about the weapons. However, the adversary works in our flesh in such a way that the combination of non-belief or the absence of faith combined with laziness causes us not to commit ourselves to what is necessary in the Spirit by a denial of the flesh to realize the victory in every area of our lives. Satan cares nothing about our energy level as it pertains to praising. Most of us can praise with the best of them. However, the Bible does not declare in Matthew 17:21, "How does this kind go not out but by 'praise,' but it declares, "Howbeit this kind goeth not out but by PRAYER AND FASTING?"

The ultimate question in the Spirit as it pertains to achieving in the Holy Spirit is, what will you do to move the devil? Praising moves God, but praising will not necessarily move Satan. It is not God who is withholding the evidence of his promises in our lives. It is not God who is keeping us from receiving the promises that have been revealed to us through the unctions of the Holy Spirit, yet our eyes are never seeing them. But it is the enemy, Satan, who is intent on robbing us of the faith that we need to properly sustain the hope and fight for what God said was ours. As long as we continue to be well exercised in the flesh and in the charismatic things that accompany serving God, we will continue to miss God. It is only when we place a greater value on what Satan is taking from us that we become vigilant enough in the Spirit to fight back in the manner that you are being fought. Oftentimes, we find ourselves waiting for God to give us something that he has already given us. We are waiting for God to bring us something that he has already brought us. Not understanding that what we are waiting for has already been delivered, but the enemy has stolen it. If you are waiting for the ability to achieve and to obtain, the Bible makes it clear that God has already given you the power to obtain wealth. Before wealth materializes in the flesh, it is provoked by faith and presented in the Spirit. This is evidenced by times where you feel like you are blessed. You unwittingly start doing the things that serve to bring the blessing into materialization. To God be the Glory! The gift of the feeling of a blessing provoked a prolific praise from you that constituted the substance of things hoped for and the evidence of things not seen, which qualifies as faith and solidifies the saying, "When the praises go up, the blessing come down." You had this inclination that God was about to do something; it has not happened yet, but you started talking about it. There is a faith thing going on. There is something happening in the Spirit realm. That's when the enemy get's busy. That's when the unexpected starts to be made evident. Things begin to break down. That's when your money stops being enough to cover the cost. And if you are not careful, you will lose that feeling, and if you are not careful, you stop doing what must be done in this realm to provoke a move of God in the unseen one. And not long after you stop giving God what the Word of God prescribes as the essentials for a move of God, the spiritual remnants of a move of God dissipates due to lack of faith. You never get the opportunity to see the blessing of the Lord for that season in the place where you dwell. In your dwelling place. Be it on the mountain or in the valley. It really doesn't matter where you are according to the seasons of your life when you see God, for to be in his presence, there is a fullness that you cannot come to know anywhere else. And ultimately, it is all about getting into his presence and realizing him. It is not as much about up or down as you might imagine. Isn't that a mystery? That very place where you need to see or you need to see it to believe God for more cannot materialize until you have the ability to bless God before it gets there. All of this has to be done "in time" to receive both the gift and the giver. You receive the giver when you not only realize what you needed to overcome the obstacle, but you also come into the knowledge of what it was all about. The course is PAR to DUE SEASON. A delayed blessing received out of *due season* is not a blessing but *defeat realized*. It is what you needed in a time where it is too late to sustain what you needed it for. It is an open reminder of what could have been. God is not a "could have been" God. He is an on-time, more-than-enough God; however, the just must learn to live by faith. What happens when you lose or if you never get the feeling? What constitutes a praise from a vessel that is not prompted by the Spirit to give a much-deserved praise? What constitutes worship beyond a feeling? KNOWING constitutes a praise before you see the thing you desire! So if it is not in you to give God glory before you see it, you will never praise him for it, and you will never see it, meaning you will never fully realize that thing that you desired, even if you deserve it. That's a mystery. But you can praise him before you see it, and you can praise him through the storm for there will come a storm if you praise God for things you cannot see for the devil wants you to stop that, for that weapon of warfare is effective in prevailing in combat against him, and the objective of the enemy is to steal to kill and to destroy. So don't stop praising! When you stop praising, you cannot get where you need to be in your flesh, neither can your flesh be sustained. You cannot live in your flesh for your flesh, just like mine, is a mess! The flesh will always settle, but your spirit knows better. Your flesh is perfectly okay with ninety-nine and a half, but your spirit knows better. Your spirit in the Spirit realm knows that ninety-nine and a half will not do. Your spirit knows that if you give the ninety-nine and offend the one point, that you are guilty of the entire thing. That's why your spirit strives for perfection in the Lord, while your flesh wars against the notion or if it is even possible. The flesh is totally okay with a part of your blessing and a portion of your birthright in God.

Until the people of God matriculate to a place beyond singing and the clapping of hands and dancing and just out and out charismatic expression alone to a place that is also inclusive of exercising faith and trusting in God with their entire heart and mind, their sensory perception will fail them every time. EVERY TIME! This old, low, down devil that you are fighting knows you well enough to know when to back off; he does not back off because he cares or because he loves you but because he WANTS YOU! He knows when you are close to your breaking point. His objective is to cause you to believe that what you are trying to conjure in your flesh is working.

So we come to a place where we find that the weapons of our warfare are not carnal. The contradiction is that your perception of your warfare *is* carnal. The mistake is in fighting what you are going through based on how you saw it. And that is the trick of Satan. That is a huge revelation. One worthy of God's anointed. This knowledge of the mysteries of God will cause you to walk in areas where things can be birthed in the very midst of where you are. Why? Because through this understanding of the things of God, we are binding up laziness in the Spirit. We have it all wrong. Churches everywhere spend exorbitant amounts of time pumping people up to praise God and to approach him in worship when all those things are superficial. They are outward expressions that do not necessarily denote true relationship with God. Yes, they will move God, but they will not move Satan. Your praise will not move Satan. However, there is something that will move Satan. There are some things to be realized that will go far beyond your reasoning. There are some things that will go beyond the explanations that you give others that make perfect sense to you and to them. There are some things that will break the laws of nature and will transcend your present circumstances. There are some things that will absolutely lead the believer into a supernatural realm and place in God that demands that he/she line up with God's will and his purpose for their lives. Those "some things" that I am referring to here are more than just simple undertakings. But they speak to understand the power found in the weapons of fasting and prayer, the consistency to be had in true dedication to worship and heartfelt relationship with God. They are also found in a practice and exercising of faith to be had in hope forecasting and faith broadcasting. All of these weapons work to strengthen the consistency of the believer's presentation to God; they also work to bolster the believer's willingness to endure hardness as a good soldier for God. All of this works to endow the believer with a knowledge of how to tap into the mystery that says, "The joy of the Lord is MY strength."

So there again, when the thief steals, he takes what you knew you had. Naturally speaking, the only reason the victim recognizes the presence of a thief is because he realizes the absence of his possessions. Someway, somehow, the victimized has taken inventory and knows what is in his possession. Now, if there is no sign of forced entry, then the evidence supports the notion that the altercation had to have been an inside job. Spiritually, the disappointment we discern in our hearts as it concerns where we find ourselves in life is oftentimes the byproduct of hope colliding with reality and faith failing to renew—not understanding that God has long released in the Spirit what we need to prosper in him and in life, not withstanding that the enemy stole or distorted under the cloak of the lack of knowledge our sustainability and increase in the Spirit (the promises of God) and disguised his manifestation in our flesh as something less than desirable (we missed the move of God). A switch and bait. He is working to bait you to nonbelief. He is working to build a legacy of nonbelief in you. What a way to try and build a relationship. Satan knows that it is faith and belief that motivates God toward us. And he understands that your relationship with God cannot be any greater than your commitment to believing in him. We are only dangerous to Satan when our faith has placed us in God's presence for it is at that very moment that we cease to walk after the flesh but after the Spirit. DANGEROUS!

Our victimization in the Spirit is an inside job. One of the weapons that the enemy uses against the people of God, of course, is lack of knowledge. Oftentimes, we just do not know, and we are not walking in a level of desire in the Lord and obedience to the Lord to receive the direction he has sent to us to find out. Disobedience/ lack of discernment are also weapons that the enemy uses against the people of God. We oftentimes have physical connections that we hold in more regard than our spiritual possibilities. We would rather play than to stay. When God sends us a word that says, "Higher," or "Get thee from amongst your kindred," or anything that you know so he can rewrite the story of your understanding and craft in you what you have never seen, we find that we are incapable of hearing his voice because of our non-commitment to doing his will. We simply fail to cast down every imagination and every high thing that exalteth itself against the knowledge of God and bringing into captivity every thought to the obedience of Christ. Lack of faith is also a key weapon that the enemy deploys against the people of God, especially those with high potential in him. The lack of faith is made evident by the lack of a sense of urgency in acting upon the instructions of the Holy Spirit. The lack of faith is best categorized by out-and-out laziness as it pertains to the essentials in God. Reading your Word, fasting, dedication, to praying in the Spirit and fulfilling one's godly duties. Whatever the reason, the end result is the same. When bound in these areas, you will not commit yourself to the victory that has already been won on your behalf.

Glory to God for his Spirit, our Comforter, for it is the Spirit of God within us who alerts us to what could be. We feel the unctions, and that is why we get disappointed with all we have ever known. Think about it. If you have never been beyond where you are, what business do you have being disappointed with where you are? Naturally speaking, you know nothing else save the Spirit of God within you who educates your ignorance beyond the borders of what is known and speaks MORE into the creases of your very soul and existence. If you have never had anything, why would you ever aspire to have more? Save the Spirit of God dictated to you that MORE is possible, but when you refuse to meet that possibility in God with your faith, then you, in essence, renege on your part of what is required to make the impossible (the non-evident) possible (evident). Manifestation is the name of the tactical offence. You have got to last long enough in faith to see what cannot be seen (but felt) manifested. Not only that, but you must absolutely relinquish your position in God when you don't. When the people of God fail to fast and pray, when the people of God refuse to hear him when he says, "Pray." Let's face it. Our God is a jealous God, and prayers that are prayed out of convenience oftentimes will not move him. "Now I Lay Me Down to Sleep" is a child's prayer and should not be found in the mouth of a seasoned trueborn believer. The time is coming and now is that those that worship him must worship him in spirit and in truth. But when the Holy Spirit prompts you, through an interruption of your sleep, to get up and seek God's face in prayer, those are the times to excel in your communion with him. The question is, do you get up? That's a weapon of your warfare that will move strong-holds and mainstays out of your life as well as the lives of your loved ones. That's a breakthrough waiting to happen. That's your way out and your way of overcoming in wait.

In this hour, we find that the people of God have grown both weary and lazy when it comes up to the things of God that will cause a move of God to burst forth in their lives. For it is in these times that we are on the cusp of things being turned around and things being rendered upside down and right side up in our lives for God. For in an effort to grow us, he begins to bear down on us that we might participate in the things necessary to bring forth the miracle that we so desperately need. So under the auspice of the enemy and when you are going through, we oftentimes will relinquish our position to the first prevailing thought that comes to our mind. For instance, the thought may be, "I need to go back to school." So you go back to school and acquire the certificates or the degrees and all the things that are very good to have but failed to do what was necessary to break that stronghold that is controlling the flow of finances and opportunity in your life, and even with the accolades, you find that you are just as despondent now as you were before you embarked upon trying to influence change. Unless you do what is necessary to break the bands of the enemy and cause the devil to let go of what God said was yours, you will never prosper because there is nothing in the halls of any institution that is classified as a weapon of warfare in the Spirit. No boss can give you anything to break the bands of the enemy. We must learn to fight the enemy on his own terms. And we cannot practice laziness in the Spirit. Learn to praise God and worship God when he begins to give you an inclination of your purpose. Learn to "lose your mind" when you know that you are going to do what is necessary to birth the plan of God out of the Spirit into the natural in your life, then when God says, "I am going to perform greatness in your life," by faith, there is nothing else for you to do but lose your mind for him in a high praise. Believing that he who promised it is more than able to perform it. Get something on your mind when you praise. Learn to praise with strategic intent, by faith. Allow your praise to usher you into the midst of the battle with the intent of inflicting damage on the enemy's position in your life, and thereby causing positive change to be experienced in the natural. Whenever and wherever you are, when you hear the Holy Spirit say, "I am going to do something awesome for you," right then, give God an, "I hear you, and I believe you praise," all the while in your spirit knowing that you are going to do what is necessary to help BIRTH this next move of God in your life. Speak a word over your life right now that says, "Come forth, in the name of Jesus."

In reproduction, ovaries do not impregnate themselves, and so it is with the promises of God in your life. There will never be a fulfilling pregnancy in the Spirit until the promises of God in your life have been seeded by your faith. Your faith has got to seed your purpose. That thing that God has dropped in you, only your faith can seed. Only your willingness to participate can impregnate. God is not in the business of raping us to get us where he desires for us to be in him. Only your willingness to participate can impregnate and eventually birth your next explosion in God.

Promise yourself even now that you are going to do better in obeying the voice of the Lord. Take note that you are tired of being robbed and molested by the enemy and that you are committed to doing whatever it might take in the Lord to achieve your next level in him. "No weapon formed against you shall prosper." Fighting is a mentality; our mentality has got to be one whereby we refuse to accept defeat even when it is clear we have suffered loss. "Hope against hope." Our consolation here is that the enemy has never properly defeated us at any time. Because through it all and in the midst of it all, we have learned more about the weapons of our warfare, and we have come to find that our obedience to the things of God is better than any sacrifice we could ever make. We refuse to concede defeat at any time, any place, and anywhere ever in our lives to the devil. Satan's biggest advantage has always been our ignorance of God, and our greatest opportunity for totally defeating him in our lives is our growing knowledge in God. So with that in mind, revisit your last defeat and consider that Satan did not defeat you but in essence you defeated yourself. Because truthfully, you did not do all the praying you could have done. You did not do all the fasting you could have done. You didn't read the scriptures nor did you seek God's face nor did you remove media devices, including the television from your spiritual diet. For there were times that the Spirit of the Lord prompted you to get up and pray and you failed to do so.

There were times when the Spirit of the Most High God told you to turn your plate down and you failed to do so. And in some cases, you did not even try. For Satan has the same lines just refurbished for different conversations. For before many of us got saved, Satan worked to convince us that we needed to wait until we were sure for "we did not want to play with God," and we certainly did not want to be hypocrites. And God used someone to help us see that we could not save ourselves anyway and that God had an expectation of us that we TRY! It was also made clear to you that if you draw near to him, he would draw near unto you. So you took a step, and now you are saved. So now when it comes down to FASTING, that same devil will tell you, "Don't you do it because you might not be able to hold out. Don't even start it. You know how you are, so it is better that you not even start than for you to start it and not finish it." THAT'S SATAN for if you start it; God is able to help you finish it.

So as you embark upon bringing a gun, not just any gun but a spiritual cannon to this spiritual fight, you will begin to experience victories that the enemy has been collecting from you. He has been stealing your mail. He has been collecting your stuff. He has been ambushing your stagecoach. He has been taking what God said was yours. He has been painting a facade that God is behind the times of lack in your life. He has put out a false image of God that we have a need to pray that God does stuff for us after we get into a dilemma. He has been trying to diminish God's authority by making it appear that God is not an on-time God. The truth of the matter is that your God knows what you stand in need of even before you ask him. And by the time you see it late, it is a restoration of a blessing distorted by the enemy. The Spirit of the Lord is fighting a battle for us called Take It Back. Our faith did not win the blessing, but God's mercy demanded that it be restored, absent of our faith. That is a blessing born out of grace and mercy. That is a blessing born out of God's love for you and not your love for God. God's love for you is a mercy blessing. Your love for God will cause your coffers not to be large enough to receive what he has in store for you. When God is motivated by your faith, you become the apple of his eye. And he begins to do things for you that you could have never imagined. He begins the process of taking you from the field, still smelling like onions and not looking like a king, and he will place you in the palace and in king's garments because of your love for him. It's time now to stop just making it off of God's love for us and learn to walk in a place where God recognizes you by your love for him. Love for God is the place in God where awesome things just fall in your lap.

Don't meet "hear" with "say," and don't meet "see" with "feel;" don't meet "smell" with "taste" because those are not your weapons, and they will not win you a move of God. Your weapons are not carnal; however, they are mighty through God to the pulling down to the snatching down, to the peeling away, to the removing, to the kicking out, to the turning over, and to the turning around of strong-holds. I dare you to proclaim right now and right where you are, "It's mine." Satan declared that it was not yours, but through the grace that is found in Jesus Christ, it is yours. Whose report shall you believe? Shake your head, and get the devil out of your mind.

> "Casting down imaginations, and every high thing that exalteth itself against the knowledge of God, and bringing into captivity every thought to the obedience of Christ" (2 Corinthians 2:5).

Make up in your mind that whatever you have got to do to get free, you are going to do it. Casting down every high thing that exalteth itself against WHAT YOU KNOW! Where do you know it at? You know it in your spiritual repository. Know nothing by or in the flesh for you can't keep or save anything of lasting consequence in your flesh. If your knowledge of God is in your flesh, you are already in trouble for your carnal mind is the devil's playground. Your knowledge of God has got to surpass your carnal opinion of who he is. Your knowledge of God must be built by faith, consummated by experience, and kept in your spiritual repository where worm nor moth can spoil it. Place your knowledge of God right next to your love for God in your repository. Your love for God must supersede all else. Choose to believe and be led by what you know. You must be convinced by your faith not to deviate from what you know God told you. And when you get weak and in times when you are not as sturdy in your faith as you know you should be, God will do what is necessary, or he will direct you as to what to do to be reestablished and to be restrengthened in the faith. There again, fasting is key because it will enable the Spirit Man to overtake the flesh when the flesh has been empowered to abound. In times when your flesh is getting too strong for you to handle and it has built up a resistance to your walk with God and your faith, fasting will serve to break down the flesh. In times when the flesh is fighting against what God has spoken into your spirit, it is imperative that you weaken the flesh to give the Spirit Man the advantage that it needs to prevail in the war between the spirit and the flesh that continues within all of us. Don't just sit there. Do something about your flesh! Thinking about doing wrong? Feel like you are about to give up? Feel like you are about to lose your position in God? Feel yourself slipping in God? Feel your commitment to the things of God whining? YOU HAD BETTER DO SOMETHING ABOUT YOUR FLESH! For the flesh and the spirit warreth against one another, and if you do not strengthen the one or the other, one of the two will suffer loss. The true issue here is your flesh or the love of the flesh is enmity to God. You have got to get it out. The Word does not say, "Ease down the imagination." It does not say, "Place down the imagination." It implies that to be successful in your endeavor to overcome, you must get violent and CAST DOWN imaginations. This thought reflects the understanding found in Matthew 11:12, "And from the days of John the Baptist until now the kingdom of heaven suffereth violence, and the violent take it by force."

Reach up, and grab it. TAKE IT BY FORCE! Tell yourself, "I have got to get myself together! I have got to. I must." Many people remain functional in the midst of dysfunctionality. They may look like they are in with you, but they are not quite right or their "regular self" in God. Our heads can be torn all to pieces. Our minds can be in another place. Sometimes, it can be a struggle to do the simplest task in God (like just making it to services). Cast it down! Cast down every imagination that exalteth itself against your knowledge of Jesus Christ! In the bosom of your soul, you know better! Cast it down! Tell it. Make it known now. Recommit it in the Spirit that you are through being robbed. Speak a prophetic word over your own life that you are going to believe silently in your spirit and that you are going to quietly make some fuss, and I am going to discretely release a scream in the Spirit the cannot be heard by natural ears. And the yell that shall break forth from my spirit shall be a commitment to God and a promise to myself that the devil shall no longer victimize me and I shall no longer be ignorant to weapons of my warfare. That yell shall denote that you are finished with the inside job that the devil has come to expect from you and that if he gets in, he's going to have to break something. No longer is it an inside job. If you have to fast to overcome, then fast. If you get on a fasting regiment and start fasting like you should, weight loss would not be an issue, and losing weight in the natural will equate to gaining weight in the Spirit. Dieting and fasting are not one and the same. Dieting attends to the things of the flesh while fasting attends to the things of the Spirit that also cover the flesh. Dieting cannot benefit the spirit; however, fasting benefits the mind, body, and spirit. Fasting requires that your intentions be turned towards God if you intend for him to put his on you. It is time to move and shake some stuff up and loose in your life. Ask God to release you in the Spirit such that your mind and the jaws of your mouth might be released to relish in, and speak those things that the Lord has unctioned was yours. Stand up in your purpose and be who you shall become! Open your mouth and tell God that you believe everything he has unctioned concerning you and what you shall be. Step out and proclaim the joys of the Lord by faith. I feel an unction to pray for you now; in the name of Jesus, I pray that the anointing of God that is in this room with me now as I write these words leaps from the pages of this book and positively changes the life of the reader in a manner that brings increased clarity to the nature of the fight that they are now engaged in. I also pray that the yokes be broken and the enemy be defeated in their lives – amen. Thank God for your knowledge of your warfare in the Spirit to this point for your knowledge has been enough to keep the issues that drive disappointment in your life from overtaking you. So your praise is in tack, and you still have your joy, but Jesus is saying he wants your joy to be complete in him. Complete joy. Complete joy is different from *some* joy. Complete joy is when you recognize and understand where you are as it pertains to God's plan for your life and debilitating disappointment is no longer a part of you because God has shared with you that all things are done decently and in order according to his will and his purpose for your life. Speak a word over yourself right now that says, "I am through being robbed." When your natural house is robbed, there are two basic things that the violated will do. First, you address the physical exposures. You will work to sure up the house, especially at the point of entry. Second, you work to shore up the psychological exposures that led to the physical invasion. You realize that the invader found comfort in knowing that no one was home at the time of the invasion. So going forward, when you leave home, you leave on lights or you leave the radio or television on so if the crook comes back, before he actually kicks the door in, he can hear what he would think is someone on the inside of the house. This is all in an effort to influence the actions of a would-be robber. In the Spirit, we can also employ the physical by utilizing our praise and our worship. We can also employ the physiological, which is the banner of the Holy Spirit that is across our lives, doing everything within our power to achieve what God has for us and no longer being active participants in being raped, seduced, and molested by the devil. Draw off of your experiences and the things that God has taught you that you might be able to come into a place of perfection now so those things that you have perceived in your heart that were brought on by your faith might begin to materialize in the flesh. Seek God's face for a sense of urgency in the Spirit, fight to wake up out of your sleep, and refuse to be in a tranquil state as it relates to achieving your designed place in God. Now is the acceptable time to achieve the promises of God in your life. You do not have the next thirty years to not achieve your purpose. Don't despise humble beginnings. Little becomes much when you place it in the Master's hands. Fight to live out every creed, every jolt, and every title of the purpose God has declared for you. NOW IS THE TIME! It's time now. It's time to pray. It's time to fast. It's time to seek the Lord's face. And he will cause it to come to past. THIS KIND GOES ONLY BY FASTING AND PRAYING! Know now and claim that you have grown up in God. Stand up and declare that you are at an impasse in your life and that you are standing next to a glass ceiling that must be breached. Declare that the grace of God has carried you up until now and that you know that, aided by your willingness to serve, there is nothing that you cannot achieve in him. This next place, this next step or phase in your evolution as a child of God, comes only by *fasting* and *praying*. Commutable, collaborative, specified fasting and praying. In this, you will see things happen, and there will also be things happening on your behalf that cannot be seen outside of the Spirit. Things will begin to break in the Spirit, and things will begin to turn around in the spirit. Fight, fight, fight! To achieve this level of liberty, you must become a student of how to *Fight* the devil on his own terms.

# Hope

"Who against hope believed in hope, that he might become the father of many nations; according to that which was spoken, 'So shall thy seed be'" (Romans 4:18).

We cannot hope to please God without faith. We cannot do anything without faith. The Bible goes so far as to say it is impossible to please God without faith. Now there are different levels of faith. There are different entry and exit points into and out of faith; however, no matter where you are, what you are doing, or whatever you are dealing with, you cannot "hope" to please God without faith. In the book of Hebrews, the eleventh chapter, there is the usage of "by faith" some twenty times. All the people and things that are referenced in that passage were accomplished by faith. They were not accomplished "by doing," but "by faith," the people of God were able to accomplish them. Faith has to lead. Before the issue is revealed, faith has to already be there. If faith does not precede you in the unfolding of events, then the task becomes one of catching up and untimely suffering. Faith precedes you, and hope precedes faith. Everything that is ordained to happen on the behalf of the people of God is going to be provoked to come to pass by faith and made evident prime for manifestation by hope. This is primarily why the enemy spends so much time browbeating the people of God and beating up on the people of God, because he desires for the people to be devoid of hope.

It is important to recognize that there are many different levels of hope. Of course, you have your personal life. You have family events both immediate and at large that raise concerns you have for your health and finances, all different types of things you may need; however, if you do not have hope, there is nowhere for faith to enter in. For hope is the bucket, and faith is the funnel from which it flows. The stream that is faith is no more than concentrated hope that penetrated the boundaries of the imagined (Spirit realm) and manifested in the natural, springing forth from the lake of hope. No wonder the scriptures read in 1 John 3:3 that every man that hath this hope in him purifieth himself even as he is pure. Hope refreshes and prepares the soul and mind of the believer for the battle. So the enemy will major at warring against you in the area of your hope. He wants to fill your mind with realisms that make so much sense to you that it becomes almost contradictory for you to believe anything other than what your senses dictate to you to be true. Simply because of a lot of the things that God desires to do for us at this stage of our walk with him we have never seen done before, and if it is going to happen, it must be built out of some great hope. We must have hope beyond hope. The simple truth of the matter is, either God is real or he is not. We can go into millions of different variations of believing, but at the heart of it all is a simple question, and that is, is God real? At the end of the day, there are one or two things that we must get straightened out in our minds and in our hearts concerning our God, and they are either he is real or he is not. The Bible declares that God is a spirit and they who worship him must worship him in spirit and in truth (John 4:24). Now, if at the conclusion of your God evaluation you find that he is real, then you MUST trust him. If he is real to you, then you have got to TRUST HIM! If he is real to you, you have got to TRUST HIM! And when we really get that down, you begin to realize how important it is for you to grow in the space wherein you find yourself and you begin to long for God to move you to heights unknown as you seek his face to take you to different levels in him. You begin to realize in the Spirit that it is imperative that you grow beyond just where you are or have been. The Bible declares, "Blessed are they, which do hunger, and thirst after righteousness: for they shall be filled" (Matthew 5:6). It is important to catch the revelation that when we say we trust God, our trust must not be limited to just where we are at that present time. Oftentimes, we war within ourselves just to come to a sustaining faith that allows us to trust God for where we presently find ourselves as it relates to all of the emotions, conditions, and circumstances that come along with our present conditions. But this trust must transcend present conditions and speak to non-directional trust. A trust that rebuts the need for immediate gratification and demands order in our minds and a prevailing stance in our spirits that says, "And we know that "all things work together for good to them that love God, to them who are the called according to his purpose" (Romans 8:28). It is also important to note that hope reaches far beyond trust in that it projects you into a space that claims the promises of God and the unctions of the Holy Spirit that are not evident at the time of your realization. Your reality has to take a back seat to your hope in the Lord. On top of all this is the knowledge that you can spend the rest of your life just trusting God to sustain you. You can spend the rest of your life just believing God to make a way for you where you find yourself presently. However, once you come to terms with the fact of how real God is, how much he means to you, how big/large of a part he plays in your life as it stands, then it becomes essential that you go to a place in him BY FAITH, whereby you HOPE beyond where you are. From there, a different type of reasoning is born that asks the question, "Why not?" Why won't God do this for me? Why not? He has done everything I have asked and, better yet, expected him to do for me where I am, and now, I am going to believe God beyond where I am. Believer, this is a totally different dispensation of faith. When you spend all your time simply believing God to help you not to be laid off or to keep the job that you have, there is not much room for believing him for a better job. When in your mind it takes every ounce of faith that you have to trust God that your check is going to be in the mailbox in time enough for you to pay the rent before that lady begins to cut up, where is there room to be trusting God beyond that, for a better place to live? Believing beyond where you are requires HOPE. So we find that oftentimes we have sustaining faith galore but not much room for hope. Oftentimes, we are guilty of trusting, not hoping. It is important to note that Romans 5:3–5 says "And not only so, but we glory in tribulations also: knowing that tribulation worketh patience; And patience, experience; and experience, hope: And hope maketh not ashamed; because the love of God is shed abroad in our hearts by the Holy Ghost which is given unto us."

Anything born short of hope is a sustaining approach relationship with God. Our focus today is on believing God beyond just sustenance. We are now entering into a place that through hope, by faith, we have drawn the conclusion that God is going to sustain you because he has placed you where you are; and now, I am believing God beyond hope. I am going to believe God beyond where I presently find myself. By faith, I am not going to be ridiculous for I am standing in a place where I absolutely believe God for what I have imagined in my mind that was born of my spirit. I believe that it is possible for my mortgage to be paid off before I am too old to enjoy it. I absolutely believe that God will save all of my children and that one day I am going to sit back and watch them go forward in the things of him. I absolutely believe that God is able to help me to live up to my full potential in him. I absolutely believe these things of God so much that I am not afraid to rehearse them aloud in my own company. Practice saying things to yourself concerning yourself. My testimony will not just be limited to where I have been but will begin to speak to where I am going through Christ Jesus. "My soul shall make her boast in the Lord." By faith, I commit to speaking futuristically in an effort to move beyond where I presently find myself, those immediate needs and desires, but now, I am believing God beyond the boundaries of where I am and where I have ever been. You must actively engage in living by faith and hope. A Jabez approach to life that says, "God, by hope not just faith, I believe and press to an enlargement in you." For you have come to understand that faith is sustaining you where you are while hope is going to take you to another place. And when you hope yourself to your next destination in God, faith will sustain you in that newfound place. The prevailing question is: do you have hope? I know you have faith, but do you have hope? You are not hoping for what you already have for hope takes you beyond where you are. It presses you beyond the obvious. You must have something that you are hoping for. Why do you think Satan does not want the people of God hoping? Why do you think the enemy's desire is that we, as the people of God, feel it dangerous to hope? Satan does not war against your believing nearly as much as he does your hoping. Why is it common for believers to advise themselves and others to, "Honey, don't get your hopes up," or "Be careful. Don't get ahead of yourself." Both of these common sayings are in direct conflict with what we should be striving to achieve through the love that God has for us. They both imply that when you get your "hopes up," you ultimately get your feelings hurt. I have come to find that it is not the elevating of hope that hurts; it's the crash that is experienced when we fail to sustain that hope in the midst of our apparent realities.

You must get your hope up, and once it is up, you must war to keep it up. Now, whatever you are hoping for may not come to pass tomorrow; however, when it does come to pass, *it* is going to happen as a direct result of what you dared hope for—the "it" being whatever God delivers as a result of your hope that aligns with his overall purpose for your life.

Your prevailing prayer must be, "Father, please do not allow me to get in the way of what you want to do for me." Do you know how quickly and often you, by your very nature, can get in the way of God's ultimate purpose for your life? Just your personality traits that have shaped who you are can very well determine where you are. We must be willing to abandon our ideas and impulses that will deny us our next evolution in God. It is important to understand that at times we get in our own way as it pertains to where God, by his Spirit, is willing to lead us. The bottom line here is that we have so many opportunities to die in God, for if we do not die in God, we condemn ourselves to staying where we are. To be honest, we have some of the craziest ideas about the effects of success. So many ridiculous things that have been burned in our minds that could not be further from the truth. "I don't want a new car because when you get a new car, people think that you think that you have it going on so I just would rather not have one. So just give me a used car." What? These are the types of ideologies that block the necessary experimentation with hope that ultimately grows faith. There are so many idiotic pillars that the enemy has erected in our minds and our hearts that have served to shape our thought patterns such that even if God came before us and opened up the windows of heaven, we are not in position mentally and spiritually to walk into those heavenly places because we have so many invisible chains that are binding us. Certainly, in a lot of ways, this idealism has helped to shape who we are, but ultimately, they work to separate us from our true purpose, possibilities, and potential in God. An understanding that all the ways you may feel about things is not God's way. This understanding is pivotal in reaching beyond where you presently find yourself in. Just an understanding of the fallibility of your flesh could be the key to you ultimately achieving your purpose in God. Certainly, we are hostage to our old ways of thinking and our familiar approaches that the enemy has used to shape our minds. Understand that through trials, tests, opportunities, and successes, God revamps and reshapes our approach to the things and the places in which we presently find ourselves. Know that our past ushered us to our present and our present will deliver us on time into our future. If our most awesome, wonderful, amazing God did not intervene in our God development, we would condemn ourselves to the dark passageways that would never lead us to the brilliance of God's divine purpose for our lives. We would settle for any light, not having realized and not knowing the glory of the light of God that shines down on those who love him. The old hymn says, "Swing low, sweet chariot." However, without the direction and guidance of God, there is no guarantee that you would get on the chariot if it swung low enough for you to step on board simply because there may be some part of you that would cause a chariot ride to be undesirable. For instance, you may not like feathers, you may be afraid of horses, or you simply may be afraid of heights. There are many of us who are afraid of heights. We worry more about coming down than we do about getting up. My point here is that there very well may be something about the idea of what God has allowed you to be presented with that you just do not like or appreciate. However, this very accommodation has been designed by God to deliver you to your next destination in him. Your breakthrough and your move of God must be synchronized with your willingness and ability to die within yourself in the time allotted by God for the revealing of his next move in your life. If you are not ready mentally and spiritually for that next move of God in your life, then physically, you will not be able to board the vehicle that he has prepared to transport you to that next destination in him. Simply because in the time appropriated, you did not die enough within yourself to be in the proper place psychologically to receive what has been ordered for you in this season. You are ill prepared to move to your next commission in God. God does not haphazardly move us or reward us with new levels and heights and depths in him. Hebrews 11:6 declares that "but without faith it is impossible to please him: for he that cometh to God must believe that he is, and that he is a rewarder of them that diligently seek him." It is of momentous spiritual significance that we experience the higher heights and deeper depths in the Lord in the time frame that has been allocated by God that you are supposed to achieve them in. Realize that you cannot take the same old you to this brand-new place in God. Every round goes higher and higher, and to get there, you must experience change from the inside out. If you do not possess the will or the skill to adhere to God's demand for change in your life, you cannot go to this next place in him that by his Spirit God is unctioning you to. The invitation has been issued, but how will you dress?

> And he saith unto him, "Friend, how camest thou in hither not having a wedding garment?" And he was speechless. Then said the king to the servants, "Bind him hand and foot, and take him away, and cast him into outer darkness; there shall be weeping and gnashing of teeth. For many are called, but few are chosen." (Matthew 22:12–14)

That is why when God ministers to you by his Spirit, you must listen to him. God is never just dealing with you where you are. That is not his way. God is a God of preparation. God prepares his people; God strategically places his people in position such that they may be able to achieve great exploits through him and on his behalf. Understand that what you are going through now or what you are dealing with or even what may be dealing with you is actually preparing you for the next place God has intended for you in him. Determine in your heart right now that you will no longer miss God due to the lack of preparation on your part to die in your FLESH! Dying is God's way. We must die so that we might live again. The scriptures read in Mark 8:34–38

> And when he had called the people unto him with his disciples also, he said unto them, "Whosoever will come after me, let him deny himself, and take up his cross, and follow me. For whosoever will save his life shall lose it; but whosoever shall lose his life for my sake and the gospel's, the same shall save it. For what shall it profit a man, if he shall gain the whole world, and lose his own soul? Or what shall a man give in exchange for his soul? Whosoever therefore shall be ashamed of me and of my words in this adulterous and sinful generation; of him also shall the Son of man be ashamed, when he cometh in the glory of his Father with the holy angels."

So we find that it is not God's will that his people suffer loss and not progressively achieving in him. It is not his will that we spend year after year in the same place in him. Ever learning but never coming into the knowledge of the truth. God is a God of perpetual motion, and his expectation is that his people would be as well. God is a God of increase; he is a God of sustenance, innovation, and creation.

"Verily, verily, I say unto you, accept a corn of wheat fall into the ground and die, it abideth alone: but if it dies, it bringeth forth much fruit. He that loveth his life shall lose it; and he that hateth his life in this world shall keep it unto life eternal" (John 12:24–25).

We must die to ourselves. We must allow God to shape us. In every way, we are our own worst enemy or our own very best friend next to Christ. We are motivated and attracted to the same stimuli continually, except God intervenes and changes our perceptions and our convictions. He literally leads us to green pastures with his rod and his staff. He comforts in his corrections even though our chastisement at the moment of the correction may not be pleasurable unto us. One would think that adverse circumstances and situations would shape us such that we would contour our choices to reflect the wisdom of our experience. However, except for the guidance and the tutelage of the Holy Spirit, whereby we have a change of heart and mind, we would continue to make the same "type" choices in our decision-making efforts. Glory be to God for his mercy! In the purging or dying to the flesh process, the children of God cannot afford for the things that once bound them to go from being "very attractive" to being "cute." That type of self-serving sanctification will ultimately get you into trouble. When by his Spirit God allows you to see that something concerning you does not please him, your response to his will for your life must be, "Lord, help me to please you in every way." That issue of your flesh must move from a place of attraction to a place of utter disgust simply because you know God detests it and your will is to please him. Your love for God and everything concerning him, including Christ, must propel you to relish in the opportunity to please him more. Your ultimate desire must become to "grow and go" in the things of the Lord. You must understand that the growth that God has for you goes beyond your membership to a church and that the growth that God has for you goes far beyond any other relationship that you have or will ever have. The only thing that can stop your progression with your relationship with God on earth is the limits that you place on him through a physical approach to building a relationship with a spiritual God. We must seek to grow in grace. We must get hungrier for the things of God and begin to run and pant after him. As you increase your knowledge of him, your relationship with him will continue or begin to grow, and your joy in him will be made complete. The only limit to your relationship with God is…You guessed it. You! Think on this: if the Lord chose to show you ten new things about himself daily for the next one hundred years, your knowledge of him would not scratch the surface of who he really is. As a matter of fact, it would take an eternity to come into the knowledge of who he has been. Oh, the wealth to be gained by a Christ relationship with God! We simply must believe God for more. We must have faith where we are, and we must have hope beyond the place in which we find ourselves. Faith will work in the place that you currently reside; however, it is hope that will land you on the mark of your next destination in God. Your hope dissected into segments of faith that serve as pieces of manifested belief over the void of nothingness that is your reality that shall purchase your next destination in God. These pieces or steps of belief are the footings that will support you on your way to the divine purpose that has been declared over your life by God himself. From nothing, hope becomes something, and the something resides in the "now," and the "now" leads to the not seen.

"Now faith is the substance of things hoped for, the evidence of things not seen" (Hebrews 11:1).

Faith will work where you are, but hope will get you to your next destination in God! Your next destination in God is going to be purchased by hope! Faith is the substance of things hoped for. We need more hope. We oftentimes struggle so hard where we are that we only have enough faith to sustain our current position in life. Most times, we have little to no unction or knowledge to hope beyond where we are, and that is when we relegate ourselves to stay where we are presently positioned in life. The question is, what are you hoping for? Ponder on that a while as you consider this. What ultimately destroys a sponge? Dryness! A sponge was created to stay solvent. It was innovated and created to stay wet. A sponge is found serving its purpose when it is drenched, when it is trounced in liquid. However, if you were to take that same sponge and devoid it of its purpose and substance, that sponge that once had been capable of gathering liquids until filled to capacity will dry up, become hard, and eventually fall away and become dust. In this example, the sponge is fashioned after *faith*, and the liquid that fills it or fulfills it is hope. Without hope, faith crumbles and dissipates with the passing breeze of time. Once faith has been severely deprived of hope, it degrades to the point that it cannot cover the immediate needs of the faith bearer. Without hope, you only have enough God awareness to be kept where you are. We must pray and ask God to give us *exuberance* where we are. We need exuberance, excitement, and "Jesus joy" where we are. That exuberance, excitement, and joy that ultimately broods into hope will take us beyond where we are. You will not find people progressively moving in the things of God that have not been renewed in their approach to him by the purging anointing found in having enthusiasm in him and in the things concerning him. God blesses enthusiasts who are genuinely excited about the endless possibilities in him. Even blind enthusiasm is rewarded. Just the excitement about the things of God. Those who are on fire for Jesus! There is no reward for the sad, sapped sanctified. God will leave you where you are and by his grace sustain you there. However, those who have hope that dictates to the hope bearer that there is a place for them beyond where they presently find themselves shall be blessed with the "re-reward."

Satan is a liar. That's what he does. He lies and his methods of communication go far beyond what we are capable of reproducing and in some cases perceive without the help of the Holy Spirit himself. When referring to people, to say he or she tells lies is to say that an individual uses their mouth to verbalize an untruth. However, when you say that Satan tells lies, if you fashion in your mind that the only means that Satan has at his disposal to predicate a lie is through a verbal communication, you have severely *missed it*. Satan is the prince over the power of the air. Satan works to set the atmosphere up around you to be one huge misrepresentation or lie. He misleads by offering misguided concepts to the senses of man that govern his emotions. He controls the air. Only faith can combat what is around you. Only faith can help you perceive differently those things that you feel or understand to be your reality. My god, we need Jesus! We oftentimes say, "If it walks like a duck and if it quacks like a duck, it must be a duck." Not when you are dealing with Satan. Satan will indicate to you through his devices that you are not blessed when you are standing in a cesspool of blessings simply because his mission is to kill, steal, and destroy. You are his mission. We must learn to trust God unconditionally, by any means necessary. Go back and look at your scrapbook of pictures that you have not seen in a while, lay the pictures out and look at the places on the pictures and not necessarily the faces. Lay the pictures out end to end. Look at the places depicted in the pictures. Of course, you know the people represented in the pictures, but do you remember the coffee table? How about the kitchen table? Do you remember the refrigerator that stopped cooling properly? Do you remember the car you used to drive or the absence of a car? Look at the pictures so the story can be told visibly concerning you and to you about what God has done for you and how far he has brought you and how God has kept you. How did he do it over the years? He did it by faith and hope that sustains and propels. Faith activates the sustaining power of God, while hope propels you to a spiritual brook that will eventually transport you to another place. Hope takes you beyond where you are only when you have been settled by your knowledge of the grace of God where you are. The Bible tells us in 1 Peter 5:10, "But the God of all grace, who hath called us unto his eternal glory by Christ Jesus, after that ye have suffered a while, make you perfect, stablish, strengthen, settle you."

It is utterly important that the people of God get more settled where we are. We must not find ourselves wrestling with God over where we find ourselves in life. We must settle to the point that we walk into a place whereby we actually hope against hope, examining the danger within ourselves or asking God to attend to the matters at hand while we oftentimes find ourselves in the quandary of really struggling mentally with where we find ourselves or the spiritual conflict that broods confusion found in the secret question of, "How could God allow me to get here in the first place?" You must WAR in the spirit to get to that place where you know that beyond a Shadow of a doubt God is going to do IT, that he is going to keep you for he has never let you down. We must bind up the works of Satan for they are working to send an air of disappointment into your spirit. They are working to cause you to be disappointed, and they are predicting that you should be beyond where you are now and that what is happening to and with you should not be happening to you. BUT in the name of Jesus, in his holy name, you must bind those thoughts up for they are not just thoughts but they are darts that have been skillfully aimed at your mind and spirit to stop you from entering into that place in God where by the impossible becomes possible in your life. Curse it and send it back to the pit! Be assured that we are having a Holy Spirit –purposed conversation right here and now and that God has ordained you to read this chapter at this time in your walk with him!

You now believe God for some money; you must hope God for more money. You now believe God for the rent; you must hope God for ownership. You now believe God for bus fare; you must hope God for your own car. You see how difficult it is to move beyond the faith to a place of hope? Unless you have the believing down pat, hoping is beyond your means for it is beyond our means to hope beyond where we believe. Faith will keep you, and hope will carry you beyond you present place, predicament, or truth. What are you hoping for?

# The Improbable Move Of God

God's ability to show up and show off on the behalf of his people is not just a run-of-the-mill occurrence. It is important to note that what God majors at in our lives are things that in all probability would not occur without his "divine intervention." In all honesty, his delivering power is the source of our sustainability in him. When I refer to deliverance, I am simply referring to God's uncanny knack and ability to show up, to bring to the past, to cause to be, to reveal, to drop off, or expunge, to cause to come into being. Never underestimate the awesomeness of God to show up in the nick of time and deliver. We must educate ourselves with the direction of the Holy Spirit to become students of the methods of God's intervening ability to deliver. Our connotation of the word *deliverance* here is not one that refers to those who need to be delivered from whatever demonic oppression that has them bound, but I am referring to God's ability to do IT. Whatever your IT may be, I am referring to God's ability to show up and bring it to pass and the methods he employs in doing so. We must mark God in his Holy Word to see that there have always been methods to his approach to the needs of his people as those needs relate to his purpose for their lives. No wonder the scriptures clearly remark in Romans 28:8 that "we know that all things work together for good to them that love God, to them who are the called according to his purpose."

We must become students of God's approach to doing what he has done, is doing, and will do for his people. We also must study how God involves himself, encompasses, and intertwines himself within the fabric of the lives of his people. We also must approach the interlocking influence of God in the lives of his people. Just the improbable, impossible interaction that God's spiritual attributes afford him. He is able to totally involve himself with his people all the time, wherever they might be, on any plane of existence, throughout all of creation. This is an example of how God's omnipotence (unlimited power) benefits the believer. God is omnipotent, and he is omnipresent (everywhere all the time). God knows all things, and he understands all the implications concerning what he knows. He has total understanding concerning what he knows. He is perfect in his doing, and there is no failure in him. There is none other who is better suited to orchestrate deliverance on the level that God does. When God orchestrates deliverance, he does not leave one stone unturned. When you are in the midst of a true move of God, it is an undeniable fact that when you go back and review God's method of deliverance as to how he processed the facts surrounding the circumstances of the issue of concern, it cannot be disputed that it was the hand of God that brought about your deliverance. There are things that break through, there are things that come through, but there is a distinct difference in things that just happen and the interlocking collaboration of God's delivering power. Just look at what you may have been facing at one time or another or what you are even dealing with right now. It becomes obvious that the nature of the issue leaves little to no room for mishap or mistake. Furthermore, even in your evaluation of the circumstances surrounding the situation, one would have to surmise that your deliverance was/is very improbable. However, when God gets involved, he somehow makes it known unto you that he is involved with the intricacies of the situation. Not only is he involved, but his involvement has endured before you even knew there was a situation. Oh my! It becomes obvious that the rudiments of your breakthrough lie in events thought to be unrelated to the devastation you presently face. It also becomes apparent that God had already provided you a way of escape that was just as much a part of the situation as the situation itself! Quite possibly, you could not see it from the outset; however, it becomes more and more clear that from the beginning to end, your issue was all GOD. Maybe you are dealing with something or facing something that you count of consequence even now and have not considered that very issue has been selected by God and determined to be the perfect storm to help whether you in the areas that will serve to groom you for your purpose in him. Even if you do not understand everything that you are going through now, it is important that you understand and realize that it is in times such as these that the improbable power of God, or even the improbable move of God, shows up and proves that he has been there all the time. God is in the midst of thee. He is in the midst of the things that drive your situation. He is not necessarily in your situation because "many are the afflictions of the righteous" (Psalms 34:19), and they come at the hand of the enemy, but he is driving your situation for "the Lord delivers him out of them all" (Psalms 34:19). God is driving your situation. He is not your situation; however, he is in control of your situation. He is now orchestrating the situation, he is causing things to come together for your good, and he is doing these things in a very improbable way. He is putting it all together that it might interlock such that once it is all done and over, it will make perfect sense to the beholder. Look at Exodus 2:1–3.

> And there went a man of the house of Levi, and took to wife a daughter of Levi. And the woman conceived, and bare a son: and when she saw him that he was a goodly child, she hid him three months. And when she could no longer hide him, she took for him an ark of bulrushes, and daubed it with slime and with pitch, and put the child

therein; and she laid it in the flags by the river's brink.

Very real issue. Very real problem. For if you were to read the first chapter of this book, you will find the dilemma is that the Pharaoh saw that it did not fare well with his people to have the Hebrews in their midst. He has fashioned in his mind that he will have all the male children of the Hebrews thrown in the river to stifle the progression of these people. Needless to say, this is a very real issue that is confronting the mother of Moses. It is important to note that the dilemma itself is the springboard in which God provides to be the catalyst that will spring *all* his people forth into the throes of their purpose. Truly, without the ever-present "determinations of destiny," which serve as the road maps and arteries for purpose attainment, there would be no God achievement in his people. So we find that our trials not only come to make us strong, but they come to help us obtain what is ours in the Lord. That is why each purpose in God for his people is different, simply because the road map that God chooses to get us to that designed place in him is just as diverse. Look at the scripture found in Romans 8:28–31.

> And we know that all things work together for good to them that love God, to them who are the called according to his purpose. For whom he did foreknow, he also did predestinate to be conformed to the image of his Son, that he might be the firstborn among many brethren. Moreover, whom he did predestinate, them he also called: and whom he called, them he also justified: and whom he justified, them he also glorified. What shall we then say to these things? If God be for us, who can be against us?

God assigns these "determinations of destiny" to the life of the believer before his birth. They serve to isolate, separate, and eventually conform the converted to the image of Christ. A child of God's approach to life, in essence, places him or her at odds with certain aspects of life. However, by his divine plan, God transforms the indifference that a child of God has with the systems, circumstances, issues, and matters that present themselves into jaw dropping, all-en-compassing *justifications* from God to promote and reveal those pre-determined places in him. It is these justifications that come together to expose God's ultimate *purpose* for your life. You must understand that it is these "determinations of destiny" by God that are must-haves for the unfolding of our "ultimate purpose" in him. In this "ultimate purpose" lies the answer to the question of "Why was I born?" These "determinations of destiny" are so eternally important because they are appointments or predestinations set up by God before the foundation of time itself had been established. They were established to deliver God's people to their destinations relevant to their purpose ON TIME!

In the true nature of the irony found in the way God intervenes in the lives of his people, the mother of Moses was unctioned by what she did not know, and no doubt could not explain, to indeed throw the child in the river, not withstanding, in a vehicle built to sustain and float on the water. Only God can cause you to see your answer in your question. Oftentimes, the door that leads to your next destination in God is found in the last place that you would look. No dilemma, no deliverer. It is the indifference of her will and obedience to the insight of God that allowed this moment of time to fulfill its proper place in destiny as it worked toward God's purpose to free his people. The duplicity of her problem was created by her unwillingness to comply. Her belief that the child was too good to die gave way for a "work around" or detour by the reasoning of God that was designed to fulfill this cog in the wheel of God's ultimate plan. Destiny is to purpose what pegs are to a wagon wheel. The measure of destiny bare the weight and forms the shape that purpose will take to fulfill God's plan. It is important to note that if God has anything, he has time, and he is a master at using it to fulfill his divine purpose in the lives of his people. You may not be able to see what God is doing, but do know he is doing something and that something he is doing is working out for your good.

So we find that the water that was to be the death of the child became the method in which God's plan for a people was unfolded and revealed. I would venture to say that the mother of Moses may have felt inclined by what she thought to believe was of her own devices, not knowing that she was being led by the determining hand of God all the while. Isn't it awesome how he leads us from time to time even when we do not understand that he is there? Never doubt the way in which God leads you for even when it appears that you have lost, you win. So here again, we are talking about the methods of God. We are talking about the improbable way that God intervenes for his people. We are also talking about provoking God to move for you in situations where you do not see where or how your breakthrough is going to come through. The first place you have got to come to is "never give up" and always be found doing all you can about what is facing you. Don't give up mentally even if you are exhausted physically. You cannot sit on the stool of "do nothing" even when you don't see or recognize God in the midst of your situation. This understanding will be the number one task that you must accept on your way to your determined end by God.

The mother of Moses was faced with a dilemma (think about your dilemmas). This woman did not give up on herself, and she did not give up on her baby. The subject of her impregnation. If you do not believe in what God has had you impregnated with, no one will. You are the first defender of your purpose in God. If you will not fight physically, mentally, and spiritually within and outside of yourself for who God is and where he has spoken you are and will be in him, then who will? You must subscribe to what the Spirit of God has ministered to you about your God and yourself in him. Moses's mother would not give up on what God birthed through her. She not only refused to give in to the reality of trial all around her, but she prepared an unanticipated method of delivery to salvage the dream of greatness that she understood concerning the gift of God. There was no way that she could have imagined that a pitched basket would play a part in resolving the unforeseen events that surrounded her blessing. But her willingness to believe that the inevitable was not the conclusion to this matter prepared her for an unction from an unseen God that led to his purpose for the child being revealed. DON'T EVER GIVE UP! How willing are you to work to assure that your destiny leads to the purpose that God has intended for your life. The woman had to lay the baby aside and work at building a basket pitched with tar that would float on the troubled tide of the Nile. At some point, she made protecting the baby her top priority. Driven by the hand of God, she made protecting the gift more important than possessing the gift. As you go through the determined rudiments of your destiny, remember to protect the gift. It is not you that the enemy is after; it is the gift of God that lies within you. If you allow the enemy to cause you to hide the gift within yourself because of the pressures of life or because you just don't feel like going forward, he will search you out and destroy you, thereby destroying the gift of God for the people of God that lies within you. However, when you think about protecting the gift and the longevity of the gift and are willing to share the gift, it is spread abroad and is impossible to locate and destroy because of where it resides, which is outside of yourself. This can no longer be about you, even in your mind. If you prepare the way by faith and an undying commitment to being what God has called you to be, he will show up! Do know that when God does show up, not only is he going to show out, but he is going to work out! When God works out, the improbable comes together. When most people get depressed or frustrated, they sit down and fold their arms and do absolutely nothing. They miss the scripture where it says, "Faith without works is dead" (James 2:17), and they begin to reflect a dead demeanor to match the deadness or absence of hope that lies within them. That is a sure way to lose; it is a sure way to end up empty-handed. You must know as Moses's mother knew, that your seed is anointed from the womb to fruition. The awesomeness of the dilemma is that God chose her to be the mother of the seed. Why? The blessing to that question lies in the answer. Long before being impregnated with the deliverer, she had been impregnated with the gift of profound determination to overcome. This is a key point factor as to why a child of God cannot afford to forsake what they are in an effort to be like those they admire. No doubt her stubbornness was an attribute that oftentimes set her apart from others or caused her great discomfort, but it is this very attribute that in this situation would allow her to rise to the occasion that shaped both her and her son's destiny, which would eventually elevate him to his greater purpose in God. Just a will to fight. Do you have that will? If you do, it is a God-given attribute, especially in the light of all that you have gone through. Ordinarily, there would be no fight, only surrender. However, in your case, you are coming out with a praise!

Moses is going to be the deliverer, but without this woman, there would be no deliverer. Just as God chose Moses, he chose this woman to be his mother. He chose her because of what he had aforetime placed in her to prepare the way for his ultimate plan. She was perfect for the mission set before her by God because of where she had arrived within the evolution of her personal growth at the crucial designated time of God's intricate, synchronized purpose in motion. Get there! We do not know if she was God's first option to carry out his plan or if she was an Elisha to someone's Elijah, but what we do know is that she was in the right place at the right time mentally, physically, and spiritually, to be used by God in a very special way. I believe that many of us exempt ourselves from being God's go-to option in key moments due to imbalances in one or more of these areas in our lives (mental, physical, or spiritual). We must know and remember that God is always prepared to win and failure is never an option with him. If not you, then God will certainly use someone else who will submit to his will and his way in a manner that is pleasing to him. A very fruitful prayer for you is very simple, "God, why did you choose me?" Do know that from the outset of things, Moses is not in any position to defend himself. Ultimately, he was going to grow to be a force to be reckoned with, but until that time, he must be faithfully guarded and protected. No wonder the Bible asked the question in Zechariah 4:10, "For who hath despised the day of small things?"

For out of the bowels of insignificance leaps forward the evidences of God's divine providence. Are you willing to fight for the gift of God in you while it is yet in its infancy? I mean, fight and stand guard over it, trusting and believing that in time, that very thing that you have defended, proclaimed, been motivated by, and stood on will come to fruition and take its rightful place in your life, proving you and doing that thing it was birthed forth in you to do? So right now, you may not be that great prophet or that great preacher or that great missionary, but the point of your focus must be directed to why God chose you for the calling in the first place. The answer will come back that you are the gift and the gift is you. The question is, what part of who you have been created to be will you allow to govern who you actually are? "For where your treasure is, there your heart will be also" (Luke 12:34), "and a man's gift makes room for him [you] and bringeth him before great men" (Proverbs 18:16). You must place a greater emphasis on who you are in God and by the wisdom found in him learn how to incorporate that understanding into your everyday life. Be assured that God's process of selection is such that just any old body cannot be anointed with the gifts of God and expect that gift to just haphazardly mature into that mandate of destiny and armor bearer of God's purpose that he designed it to be. No, we are vetted by our trials and our fortitude by faith to overcome them. For without faith—not the gifting, but faith—it is impossible to please God (Hebrews 11:6). It is important to note that only fighters make it to maturity. Only those who dare defy the odds inevitably find themselves in that improbable place in God, achieving those things that outside of the influence of God could never have been achieved. That *special* place in God, reserved for the *special* people of God. All separated by others by their ability to live or walk out faith. The Bible explains it this way in Matthew 22:14: "For many are called, but few are chosen."

The calling precedes the assignment. The assignment is given once the selection process has been completed, and you have been chosen. After being chosen, Moses's mother did all she could do when she constructed the basket, daubed it with slime and pitch, and placed it on the water. God was in the water and took it from there. When you do all that has been placed in you by God to do, he will take it from there. God's plan does not start nor end with us. We must understand that God has planned beyond what we can see. It is important to note that when you are sitting at home listening to a crying baby, worrying about what Pharaoh is going to do, you cannot see the river. However, God is in the waters of the river, and if you never place your basket on the water, you will never be able to take advantage of the ripples that God has provided to guide you to your purpose in him. God is saying, "I am in the ripples." So here, we find the importance of doing our part in the evolution of our gaining the victory of our purpose in God. It is not clear on that faithful day if the tides were high or low, but what is clear is that all the tides were headed directly to the king's palace. When God gets involved or when God has ordained a thing, it inevitably unfolds to the manifestation of what God has unctioned. Eventually, everything just comes together. When God is involved, there is no need for you to try and make things work or pull things together; things just work together. God is revealed in your "just so happen" times. Things end up broken when we apply pressure in our desire to make things work in ways other than God's divine purpose for them. We oftentimes find ourselves working to fit the proverbial square peg into a round opening simply because we want it to work, but we have not absolutely studied God's will for that given situation. Understand that when things are forced, they may work for a while; however, in time, they will fail simply because of the damage inflicted by the act of forcing incompatible pieces together in a manner that was never designed by God. There again, when God does it, EVERYTHING comes together and works. Look at what Jesus says in John 10:4–5, "And when he putteth forth his own sheep, he goeth before them, and the sheep follow him: for they know his voice. And a stranger will they not follow, but will flee from him: for they know not the voice of strangers."

We, as the people of God, must become students of God's methods of deliverance. We must become more sensitive to when God is moving on our behalf or using us on his. Simply, we must become better at reading the signs in the Spirit that signify when God is involved with a given situation. We must search within ourselves by objective reasoning if the results we are experiencing by our actions are the result of God's involvement or is it just us based out of our ingenuity, or are we just pulling something together for the time being, or is this God working things out to our good? The keys to remember here are, it is important to walk with God and include him in all of your decisions and ways and that it is ultimately important that we, the people of God, be obedient to his Spirit. God will always manifest himself in the midst of your obedience. It is very possible to miss God. It is also very possible to be out of sorts with God. Either one of these states will cause you not to be in the right place to possibly hear or respond to his perfect will for your life. Outside of God's perfect will resides failure; inside of his perfect will lies his purpose for your life. There is a very thin line between blessed and cursed, and that line is often called obedience to God—blind obedience, an obedience that denies your fleshly inclinations. Of course, losing her baby was not something that the mother of Moses delighted in, but there was something on the inside of her that dictated that she had to place him in the water for losing him meant his survival. Unpleasant but all God! How many blessings have we missed because we were not inclined to obey God, when his directions were in direct conflict with our own desires? Regardless of what it feels like and regardless of what things look like, we must be prepared to move in the affirmative when we believe a thing to be what God would have us to do. In this, we will, in a lot of instances, unlock the mysteries of God in our lives simply by being motivated by faith to obey the voice of God. You must work to never second-guess God. In this hour, we must become comfortable with leaning and depending on our Lord and Savior, Jesus Christ. Remember that just because you cannot hear God does not mean that he is not speaking. God, by his Spirit, is forever speaking. Oftentimes, our hearing God is contingent on our being still and watching and listening for him. God will instruct us as to what to do; however, doing nothing is never an option. Remember that faith without works is dead. In the midst of your calamity, God is engaged in an effort to grow you into that perfect place for you in him. So we find that when the Pharaoh's daughter collected what would be trash from the Nile River, a nasty basket that just so happened to catch her attention, understand that in the use of this basket, God was in the process of delivering his people. No, he did not speak from the heavens, and he did not cause the earth to shake, but it was all God, and he was involved from start to finish with this *awesome* unfolding of time and chance. God was in the *process* of delivering his people. Never discount God's process of deliverance in your life. God, through his infinite wisdom, knows exactly how to deliver your breakthrough. Through his divine providence, God causes things to be within the framework and fabric of what has already been and what seems to be in the subtleties of what is possible. God knows exactly how to place the mail in the mailbox such that it reaches you not only *on time* but *in time* to work to his ultimate purpose that lies beyond your needs. It is only when you take a step back and look at things in their totality that you can see the magnificent hand of God at work in your life. When you really take notice of the events that have come together to make up your life, you find that all the different improbabilities that have occurred overtime were orchestrated by God and have come together to forge your arrival to your purposed place in God.

# Inside Out

In keeping with the thesis or reason for this very work, it is ultimately important to remember what the scriptures teach us in Hebrews 11:6, "But without faith it is impossible to please him: for he that cometh to God must believe that he is, and that he is a rewarder of them that diligently seek him."

*Diligently* simply speaks to something done or pursued with persevering attention or painstaking effort. Understand that God, in all his infinite wisdom and tridimensional presence, is fit to judge what is in a man's heart. For the Word of God brings to bare in Hebrews 4:12–13, "For the word of God is quick, and powerful, and sharper than any two-edged sword, piercing even to the dividing asunder of soul and spirit, and of the joints and marrow, and is a discerner of the thoughts and intents of the heart. Neither is there any creature that is not manifest in his sight: but all things are naked and opened unto the eyes of him with whom we have to do."

So make no mistake about it. The Lord knows where we are, what we are doing, and what we are capable of. Look at 2 Timothy 2:19, "Nevertheless the foundation of God standeth sure, having this seal, The Lord knoweth them that are his. And, let everyone that nameth the name of Christ, depart from iniquity."

So it is fit to walk in the scriptures whereby they teach us in John 4:23 that, "But the hour cometh, and now is, when the true worshippers shall worship the Father in spirit and in truth:

for the Father seeketh such to worship him. God is a Spirit: and they that worship him must worship him in spirit and in truth."

In essence, the scriptures teach us that praise and worship is and should be a matter of the heart, and that true praise and worship should be approached from the inside out. A good question that you might ask is, when is it a good time to praise and/or worship? Well, praise is a more outward display or physical manifestation of jubilation toward God for some act of God born of his grace prompted by his mercy, while worship can be a more inward presentation unto God born of a heartfelt adorning and adoration motivated by faith and prompted by gratefulness. It speaks to a realization that has occurred within the heart and mind of the believer. Acts of worship bring up subject matter that is born of faith in God, his Word, and what we, the believer, understands that pleases him. Our willingness to act endears us to him. Meditation, intercession, dedication, tithing, and giving. Worship is oftentimes not as exuberant as praise but, its effects stirs heaven and in turn moves God. A worshiper, more times than not, goes undetected because they do not always move out in a charismatic fashion or their internal combustion does not totally consume their people facing selves, but be not deceived by the calmness of their approach to the things of God for their fire for God runs deep and is kindled by their love for him. Between the heart of a worshipper and the bosom of God, a special bond is formed. God takes personal responsibility for all things concerning a worshiper and always engrafts the worshiper in his overall plan of action. A worshiper unwittingly dedicates himself to the things of God so God knowingly dedicates himself to the matters concerning a worshipper. Every true worshipper has been blessed with a sense of naivity about life, about how things work, about why things work, about who God is, and about the role God plays in the life of the believer and the world at large. It is in this naivity that the purity of heart is found and the rudiments of being adopted by God lies. Many of us know too much and are too self-aware to walk with God as Enoch did. The Bible says that Enoch walked with God, and in time, he was found with him.

"And Enoch walked with God after he begat Methuselah three hundred years, and begat sons and daughters: And all the days of Enoch were three hundred sixty and five years: And Enoch walked with God: and he was not; for God took him" (Genesis 5:22–24).

Hebrew 11:5 says, "By faith Enoch was translated that he should not see death; and was not found, because God had translated him: for before his translation he had this testimony, that he pleased God."

Enoch's total dependence on the will of God for his life and the world at large made him useless to man but inexplicable to God. God made him, God noticed him, and God took him. Wow! There is no wonder the Bible says when we think ourselves to be something that we are nothing.

"And if any man thinks that he knoweth anything, he knoweth nothing yet as he ought to know" (1 Corinthians 8:2).

A worshipper can be found in God. A worshipper can speak a wonder or mystery right where they are and proactively dismiss anything that is occurring at that present time and can also dismiss anything contrary to the image of God in their heart that might occur in the future. True worshippers have made a conscious decision that they are going to follow God's lead for their lives and that they are going to serve him with a willingness to follow. The worshipper is able to surrender their minds and thoughts as well as their very being to God's will for their lives. The worshipper, in time, engages in a conscious decision to no longer wrestle and fight with the will of God for their lives. There is an awesome word of God to his people from a mighty man of God who suffered many things by the hands of others all the while maintaining his anointing and integrity in the Lord. David is that man. Look with me at Psalms 13:1–6.

> How long wilt thou forget me, O Lord? Forever? How long wilt thou hide thy face from me? How long shall I take counsel in my soul, having sorrow in my heart daily? How long shall mine enemy be exalted over me? Consider and hear me, O Lord my God: lighten mine eyes, lest I sleep the sleep of death; Lest mine enemy say, I have prevailed against him; and those that trouble me rejoice when I am moved. But I have trusted in thy mercy; my heart shall rejoice in thy salvation. I will sing unto the Lord, because he hath dealt bountifully with me.

It is obvious that David has suffered and is suffering great things at the time of his penning this psalm. I don't think that you can necessarily draw off of any one thing that Bible history tells us that David had gone through as the catalyst for this psalm. I believe that by this point in David's conquest to acquire the manifestation of the promise of God over his life, David is showing the cumulative effects of constant embattlement and turmoil. It is important to note from the example of this psalm that as humans, it is very possible to grow weary with the bombardment that we must endure to meet the spiritual deadlines that God has set for us along the time continuum. Even when we know and believe that he is with us and has ordered our steps, there will be moments of truth, consideration, and inquiry where we approach God in intercession in an effort to reset our body, minds, and spirits with his immediate will for our lives. So David encountered and endured a huge number of things to be made and to come into the place where God would have him to be. To David, it must have felt as if when Samuel prophesied to Jessie concerning him, that his journey began, and so did his sorrows, all the way up until God brought him into that place that he told him he would bring him to. In so many words, one could say that

David was perfectly fine on the backside of nowhere, seemingly destined to live out his days tending the herd of his father in total isolation and obscurity. So we now know that it was not until Samuel, led by the hand of God, was sent to awaken the purpose of God through and by the word of God in David's life that David started his quest toward greatness. It is so awesome that the word of God that was spoken concerning David was not spoken directly to David, but it was spoken to Jessie concerning David in the hearing of David. This secondhand conversation was enough to span the events that would eventually lead to the next king of Israel. I tell you that what you have heard concerning your place in God's plan is enough to leave you in obscurity or propel you to greatness in God. That's why it is so important to be around people who will speak the *good* things of God over your life and to you concerning who you are in God. So David was doing well until his *purpose* caught up with him. However, as soon as David's purpose caught up with him, he embarked on a journey that he did not initiate but only he, by faith, could complete. Understand that you will never reach your true destination in God until you get on the road that leads to your *purpose* in him. So David was safe in obscurity, sitting back in the pastures and in the woodlands tending the herds of his family. Safe does not lead to greatness, and greatness is not found in familiarity even though familiarity prepares you for the nuances that cause greatness to come about. Greatness is found in the midst of what you were called to do. So when David stepped into his purpose, the events that were to shape his destiny appeared to be some of the worst circumstances he could have ever imagined for himself. But just as water shapes solid granite, the influx of the changing tide of his life began to shape him as the next king of Israel. Unbeknownst to him, within the discrepancy of what had once been "the norm" for his life and what had become the "new normal" for his life lay the details of God's divine purpose for his life. It is in the crevices of what we go through that we find the evidence of where we are going to.

So in this thirteenth chapter of Psalms, we find David "just keeping it real." Most of us would not be comfortable framing a conversation with God in the manner that David frames this conversation here. Look at the first verse, "How long wilt thou forget me?" We may think in these terms, but not many of us actually say it aloud to God. This saying is totally born of relationship with God and being comfortable in that relationship. Here, David serves as an example for us and illuminates the type of relationship that is possible with the Father. David is showing us that it is perfectly okay to talk with God and to be honest with him when we pray. Understand that this question is not born of disrespect or lack of faith, but it is a question from this man of God who recognizes God as God and also embraces the fact that God has a divine purpose for his life. However, the man of God is recounting the cost in terms of forfeits and conceding and asking God how much more of this relinquishing his plan calls for. David understood the importance of aligning his will with the will of God and his divine purpose for his life. Obviously, this psalm starts out with a depiction of what quite possibly was a very low place for David. Here in the thirteenth chapter of Psalms, David has come a long way from Jessie's house and historically has a long way to go. But the consolation is found in the "right-now-ness" of this prayer. David, through the framing of this partition to God, is showing us that God is a God of "right now," and even though he is totally involved with what you will become, he is not totally consumed by it. God does care and is concerned about the effect the transitions of life guided by his divine purpose has on you. So here, David is asking God a real question out of himself or that is a total consideration of his flesh. How long? A question that originates out of the place where our *feelings* reside. That place that divides the church, you from the you that you are most of the time. The dividing depository of the you that you show people, from that you that does not understand, the you that just can't see, that you that's trying to be a good Christian but is finding it hard right now, that you that is fighting to be faithful. This is the place that we find David in, in the outset of this scripture. This is not the David that fought Goliath; this is not the David that cut a piece of the garment of Saul's. This is David absent of the heroics and absent of the demands of a particular situation. This is the vulnerable David that always existed that God fell in love with. The thing that made David so special is his ability to be afraid, concerned, and apprehensive, yet remain functional and exemplary in his service, his beliefs, and ultimately to God. So here, David asks, "How long will you forget me?" The only people truly qualified to approach God in this manner are those who are putting in work. By that, I mean those who have been there and done that and have the scars to prove it. Those saints who are doing all they know how to do and in the midst of all they are trying to put forth for God, it seems that in their time of need, that God is not prevailing. Not that he is not present, but that he is not riding high to save the day. In time, we come to understand that saving the day is not always his plan, but fulfilling his purpose in you is. So in this, we find that our emptiness in trials goes beyond just "stuff" and moves into the emptiness of not perceiving God, or even at times recognizing his presence or involvement in a given situation for long periods of time. So the not seeing God and the not realizing him is oftentimes the fulcrum of our frustration more so than the absence of things.

The sense of abandonment in the midst of a trial creates a wilderness experience that works to compound the frustration of the saint. So David rounded off his question with "Oh, Lord," a proclamation that denotes he knows exactly who he is referencing and what he is asking of him. In "Oh, Lord," David is articulating that God is his everything. He is expounding with measured words that he is all messed up and he cannot see God anywhere, and to make matters even direr, God is his everything. Sometimes, the best thing for you is a good cry that mentally, physically, and spiritually relinquishes your state of being into the hands of the

Almighty God. Even for those of us whose mental projection of our spiritual selves do not lend itself to being broken spiritually for long periods of time, we too must come to terms with the contradictions of our reality and our faith. On the one hand, the Spirit of God that lives within us has prompted us to believe that we have greater before us than where we presently find ourselves, while the reality of this natural realm works to constantly remind us that the disappointment that lies within us is not a tool used by God to drive the believer ever toward the promises of God but that it is the barometer of what we can expect going forward. So effective communication with God oftentimes boils down to speaking out in truth what has troubled your spirit. In this passage, David approaches God with a "you and me" conversation that respectfully recalls the nature of the relationship between him and his God as Lord and servant.

God's response to this heartfelt question very well could be, "Forget you, how?" Understand that David's question is the epitome of a promise yet fulfilled. For to look upon David is to look upon the promise of the Lord both to a people and on an individual level. Wow, it is something to realize that even though you bear the burden, it has never been about just you. David's time of manifestation transcends just a timing that accounts for his personal position in life, but must also be inclusive of the timing of a people and a readiness for a nation to embrace the changes that God has proposed for it. The called of God must be faithful enough to wait on God and trusting enough in him to believe that he has designed the perfect time to manifest his purpose in the audience of all those concerned.

The move of God for you or through you is not just for you; it is not just to meet some physiological need we have to be proven to those in our realm of influence or a need to be rescued from the pressures and uncertainties of life, but it is for all those whose destiny is tied to the call of God on your life. Be mindful of the scripture that details in Luke 12:48, "But he that knew not, and did commit things worthy of stripes, shall be beaten with few stripes. For unto whomsoever much is given, of him shall be much required: and to whom men have committed much, of him they will ask the more."

The Lord is performing a mighty work through you, not just by you for that indicates no real shaping of the times of your life. God is utilizing everything about you to achieve his purpose for your realm of influence. You are the instrument that he is using to set in motion his purpose for the times of your life. So here, David is asking, "When is it coming? What is the time frame?" It appears that, at this point, even David may be feeling that he has given all that he can give. Do know that honesty is the best policy? And here, the man of God is speaking out of himself. David is very human here, and he wants to know when. Think about how often we grow both weary and tired. Many may not realize it but in this act of conversing with God, David is actually communing with him and thereby worshiping him. David, in a manner oftentimes unrecognized as worship, is paying God the highest form of homage by proclaiming quite simply, "I need you now." The Spirit of the Lord does not bring us to an inward place of realization that says we need God; it is our faith in him and our belief in what he can do that does that for us. As long as you allow the frustrations of life to keep you out of the presence of God, you will miss him when you need him most. Most of the time, we do not go to God when we assume that our presentation is not one that we would be proud to present to him. We reserve our times of conjuring up God for those times when we perceive that our presentations are meat for the king. However, this is a huge mistake and an awful miscalculation on our part for it taints our offering to God as the sacrifice of Cain was tainted for it is bathed with pride and not with the pureness of heart as Able's sacrifice was. No wonder when we do not get the God response we think our offering should have won us, our countenance falls and "sin lieth at the door" (Genesis 4:7). It is pureness of heart, mind, and spirit that wins God. Look at John 4:22–24.

> Ye worship ye know not what: we know what we worship: for salvation is of the Jews. But the hour cometh, and now is, when the true worshippers shall worship the Father in spirit and in truth: for the Father seeketh such to worship him. God is a Spirit: and they that worship him must worship him in spirit and in truth.

Remember, we have our part to play in the fulfilling of God's reason for choosing us in the first place. Don't allow Satan to steal your joy. In the midst of your being made by God, don't stop being the you that got you chosen by him in the first place. In the light of this understanding, as David approached it, when is the *right* time to go into worship before the Lord? Understanding that the true sense of worship speaks to realizing God as God. The time is coming, and now is, when the true worshippers will worship God in spirit (that's your small *S* spirit) and in truth. KEEP IT REAL. So again, I ask, "When is the best time to go into worship? When is the best time to bare your all to the Lord of your salvation?" When you start the conversation of worshiping God and realizing him in "spirit and in truth," you must know that conversing with him in your private time with what is politically correct is not the manner in which to move him to a speedy response on your behalf. In this case, we are not talking about not letting your good be evil spoken of, for there is no one present but you and the Lord. In your private time, your concern does not need to appear to be a good example for other people. We are talking about coming pitifully before the throne of grace. We are talking about letting down your proverbial hair. We are talking about moving into a place where you are comfortable with bringing your all unto the Lord no matter how embarrassing, immature, complicated, or simple. The best time to worship is when you are thoroughly prepared to lay your all at the feet of God for you cannot truly worship him unless you step up in faith (that's spirit) and unless you are prepared to be honest with God and yourself. That's relationship. It is important to note that it is impossible to run game on God, for by the time you try and fix up how you feel, God already knows how you feel, and all he wants from us is the truth. Remember, God will never minister *truth* out of a *lie*.

See, you must become ever more comfortable with being totally honest with God so he can/will minister to you where you are. Your future is totally contingent upon your present and the ability your faith affords you to embrace the truths that make up the present while totally believing God for an end that does not resemble your present. Faith is not measured by one's ability to discredit the present by a barrage of misrepresentations and falsehoods, but it calls into existence a stance that says, "Even though my present is set in chaos, my future is made relevant by my confidence in God's ability to deliver on his promises. I am sane in my understanding of my now, but I am motivated by my belief in the unseen yet understood." Most people are ill prepared to deal with the evidences of the now while embracing the hope of the not yet realized. We must become encouraged enough in God to be led by the Spirit of God in the navigation of day-to-day occurrences while yet remaining motivated by his unctions through faith to reach those heights through him in life not yet realized. Most of us die in our now and never aspire by faith to what we could be. It takes faith to outlast your lot in life; to claim your place in God is determined for you by his spoken promises over your life. You have too much life ahead of you to die now! Now dying is not just a physical demise that occurs when the physical man ceases to be; it is the very moment in the mind, body, and spirit in which you cease to believe the promises of God just enough to push toward your proclaimed destiny in him. The moment you begin to take life at face value, YOU DIE. The moment you start to believe that all you have is all that life has to offer, YOU DIE. DON'T DIE NOW! You have been through too much to die now. If you were going to die, you should have done it before now!

Refuse to allow the enemy to cause you to be self-righteous in your own company. That's to say, refuse not to be able to bare all before God. Submit your pride and compromised view of the things around you, and totally surrender to his divine presence and holiness. Remember that it is by his grace that we have an audience with him and not because of our worthiness. Make the most of your private time with God. Be sure to speak things that really matter and that are relevant to where you are in life and in your walk with him. Allow your lips to birth issues before the Lord that will prompt him to breathe life into dead places within you and in your surroundings. So David's example for us simply asks of the Lord, "How long shall you forget me?" In essence, he is saying, "I am doing the best that I can." So in this dialogue, David opens up a line of communication with God that is bound to lead to some level of spiritual liberation for him. In this honest approach to God, it becomes apparent that God's desire is to deal with his people from the inside out and not from the outside in. It is an abomination before God to appear one way and be something different from the inside. God is not into how "good" you look. God deals in your innermost feelings, your thoughts. God deals in the condition of your heart. The Word of God proclaims in Hebrews 4:15, "For we have not a high priest which cannot be touched with the feeling of our infirmities; but was in all points tempted like as we are, yet without sin."

God is all in your feelings. It is important to note that God is spirit, and because he is spirit, he does not hurt in the way we as flesh know it. The closest God comes to hurt is his LOVE for you. So when you hurt, God feels your hurt through his love for you. It is this disruption of God's harmonious love for you that creates the sensation of discomfort for God that we recognize as pain. Outside of God's love for his children, God does not hurt. He hurts because he can feel your infirmity through you. This, in part, is what makes the gospel experience so special. For through Jesus Christ, God was able to live the experience of man while he himself knew no sin. Our God knows what it is to be human. Our Savior shared the human experience so mercy and grace could abound all the more over mankind through the knowledge of what it means to be you.

So as you begin to open up dialogue with God, it becomes apparent that there are only two places that you could possibly be in God right now. Either you are in God's perfect will, or you are in his permissive will. Permissive will can be provoked by your steadfastness in prayer, but it does not mean that your allowed predicament is where you should be. It is very possible to pray your way into a place that God never designed for you to be. When your desire to be supersedes your desire to please God, then oftentimes through your persistent demands and unwillingness to yield to the will of God for your life, you will find yourself in a parallel existence stuck somewhere between where you want to be and what God has purposed for your life, in a "flux" if you will. A place of discontentment, loss, and aguish. Kept by God but lost to his true purpose for your life. Devoid of peace and uneasy about life itself. To be at peace with life is to be assured that you are where you should be, doing what God has purposed you to do. A spiritual undertaking that provokes a peace that surpasses all understanding. Our faith must open our hearts to a truth that declares, "The steps of a good man are ordered by the Lord," that place that declares, "God, not my will but thou will be done." It must become more important to us that we become what God would have us to be than what our flesh works to dictate to us that we want to be. The issue here is that once we are released into God's permissive will, it becomes increasingly more difficult to discern that we are not walking in his perfect will for our lives. We fall into a place of "seem right," and our feelings drive us to a place of realizing our purposed desire through a prioritization system that places our desires above those godly aspirations we once had. We lose sight of the proficiencies and ordinations that have been assigned to us, and we chase a dream that will never fulfill the urge to achieve what God so uniquely placed in his chosen vessels. We fall into temptations designed by the enemy to separate us from the call of God over our lives. The difference in the ability to please God is as simple as realizing which will you are in. God is a "keeping" God, and he will keep you in his permissive will just as well as he will keep you in his perfect will. The difference is in his perfect will, you will achieve your true purpose, and you will please God and enjoy the pleasures realized by them that please him. Permissive will is easy, mindless, and requires little to no endurance in the faith. While walking in his perfect will requires trust, patience, long-suffering, temperance, peace, and above all else, faith. Remember, without faith, it is impossible to please God. It is up to the believer to walk in God's perfect will for their lives. Certainly, we have to seek his face and pray to walk in his perfect will. Understand that we can spend years of precious time that we can never redeem in a permissive state simply because we refuse to realize his willingness to be involved with every aspect of our lives and pray and seek him out. In permissive will, there is struggle, there is strain, there is frustration, and it only serves to disrupt the perfect balance of time and assignment for the believer in God. Being in the "flux" will deter you long enough to cause you to miss your divine appointment and alter the course of your purpose in him. God will keep you no matter which will you find yourself in; however, you must fight your way to his perfect will. So as you approach God, your heart must be open by faith whereby your desire is to be where God would have you to be, when he would have you to be there, with a commitment to deal with your flesh as necessary! It is impossible to walk in this place of heightened God awareness and be alive. You must die in your flesh to get here because everywhere you are, there are pieces of you intertwined. You must separate yourself to be able to be all that God would have you to be. If you do not die to the flesh, separating your desire from the will of God will hurt too bad to see it through. Understand that God's will is to take his people from glory to glory, to a place of elevation—not just a sustained place in him, but upward mobility in him. God's preferred method to truly bringing his children into sweet communion with him has always been, and will always be, from the Inside Out.

# Reader Testimonies

I am blessed to be the oldest sister of Apostle Mark Spell. Growing up in a household with six children, he and I were best friends and confidantes. It made a world of difference when I needed an ally that he was always by my side. Fast-forward twenty years, and I have witnessed him transform into a powerful man of God. Spiritually, our roles have reversed; no longer am I his big sister, but he has become my big brother. He has shared a wealth of knowledge, experiences, and godly insight that has been invaluable to my Christian walk. In fact, he was very instrumental in my becoming a Christian. I know this book will be a tool that God will use to impact the lives of many people. (Roylisa Mcquaig)

I actually came to the ministry in 2003. Apostle Spell is the epiphany of excellence in ministry without excuse. He cares about the souls of God's people as well as their livelihood. Apostle is not afraid to admit when he makes a mistake, and he tries his best to do right by people. What parishioners appreciate most about Apostle Spell is that he leads by example. He not only tells people to love, he shows people how to love. This is most beneficial to those who have never received love, who have difficulty showing love towards others, and who do not know how to receive love. His approach to ministry is truly unique. Apostle is respected of his colleagues in ministry as well as his coworkers.

Apostle is a man of prayer and supplication. He pushes parishioners spiritually to reach beyond what is comfortable.

Apostle is able to meet individuals on their level and then explain what people should do to attain growth in God. His laboring in the spirit for souls is most admirable. Apostle will not rest until members achieve spiritual and natural breakthrough. He does not show weakness nor indecisiveness. He embodies the essence of leadership. It is a privilege to serve in a ministry under the leadership of such a prolific teacher, dynamic speaker, and minister of the gospel as Apostle Spell. (Lasaundra Booth)

The pastor continues to mean something great in my life. God has placed a holy figure on earth that can receive a word from him that can lead and guide me to becoming a man of integrity. The process of molding me into what God wants me to be hasn't been an easy process. There have been times where I have received the pastor's instructions and guidance from God, but I have stood in my own way. The pastor has to lay the proverbial "stick" upon me, and I have taken that with acceptance because without it, I would still be in the world just wandering around like the people coming out from under the hand of Pharaoh. I thank God for what he continues to give the pastor for my spiritual growth and reaching that complete man of integrity. My daily spiritual goal is to be a servant to the man of God as the disciples were to the Son of God. I bless God for the man of God in my life. I wouldn't be able to get to the place where I am now without the pastor. The words of encouragement, confidence, and being something for God is what the pastor continues to put in my spirit. The pastor always says, "Seek God first," and "Hear from him and you cannot go wrong." He continues to push me and give correction when I know that I'm going left instead of right. I can truly say as the Son of God was to the people in the world that is what I say the pastor is to me. I must move out of my own way to move in the direction God has given the pastor to lead me. (Reggie Dickerson)

As a girl growing up, I always knew that I wanted a husband that would love God, be a hard worker, and a great father to our children, and I have all of that and more in my husband, Mark

Spell. It is a great honor to be married to someone that loves people so much that he is always willing to give all that God has given him in ministry. Holiness is definitely a lifestyle for him, and his desire to see others reach their full potential is always on his heart. Apostle Spell is a great example that God is still moving through his people in awesome ways. God is still working miracles. (Lillian Spell)

Dear Apostle,

I greet you in the matchless name of Jesus Christ. I write to you in the same form that Paul wrote to the Ephesians when he wanted to express his advice and counsel to the followers of Jesus, the Christ.

I would like to thank you for the interventions in the affairs of my life. I came to Greater Life some nine years ago, broken, barren, and on the verge of giving up. But I thank God for allowing the God in you to speak life, encourage, build me up, and love me in the ways a shepherd should love his sheep. He allowed you to take me into a deeper understanding of what it means to be a servant. Through you, I am mother of two wonderful kids. I am happier now than I've ever been in my life, and I am developing the gifts that God has given me. The seeds that you have sown in my life have taken roots and are now growing. Suffice it to say, thank you for being a "perfect" example of what it means to be a Christian.

Yours for the gospel's sake, Evangelist Shonda Parrish.

from the "Triumphant Living" series

# FRESH FIRE

*Spiritual Transitions That Lead to Total Man Rebirth*

by Mark L. Spell

## STUDY GUIDE

*"And from the days of John the Baptist until now the kingdom of heaven suffereth violence, and the violent take it by force."*
-Matthew 11:12

# Why The Tombs?

> "Howbeit Jesus suffered him not, but he saith unto him, go home to thy friends, and tell them how great things the Lord hath done for thee, and hath had compassion on thee."
>
> —Mark 5:19 (KJV)

I) Bound by Familiarity

- Discuss the significance regarding the statement "Demons are perfectly at home amongst *DEAD THINGS*"?

- The author explains that believers are not defined by what they say but by what they consistently do. Examine your actions. Identify areas of strength and target at least one area that you plan to improve upon.

- Examine at least two of the following statements:

    1. It is very possible for Christians to be bound by what USED to be.

    2. The enemy wants you to "live out your lives fighting your past so you will never get to the place whereby you can live out your future."

    3. Mood swings can be a sign of demonic possession.

II) The Nature of the Fight

- Explain why discernment is an invaluable tool for believers to have as it relates to deliverance?

- Why is it important for believers to maintain their ability to resist the devil?

III) From Graveyard to Purpose

- What benefits are afforded to believers when they cease to live in past hurts, rejections, or feelings?

- Explain how a believer's willingness to worship is key to coming out of familiarity.

# Triumphant Living: Dare To Do!

> "Then Jesus said unto them again, 'Verily verily I say unto you, I am the door of the sheep. All that ever came before me are thieves and robbers: but the sheep did hear them. I am the door: by me if any man enter in, he shall be saved and shall go in and out, and find pasture.'"
>
> —John 10:7–9 (KJV)

I) The Door Called Jesus Christ

- Discuss the power that lies within a believer's expectations. What are you expecting in Christ?

- Why is it important for believers to increase their expectations of life?

- Explain why believers must have the fortitude to believe beyond what we deserve.

II) Triumphant Living

- Stand on the Word of God

- The importance of changing your mindset.

- Don't struggle with your God identity. You've got to come to a place where you know who you are and whose you are.

III) A God of Progression

- Prepare to win!

- Discuss at least three principles covered within the chapter that will aid believers in resisting the urge to give up.

IV) Reaching the Next Level

- Examine the relationships of the following:

    1. Paul and Silas

    2. Mary, Martha, Jesus, and Lazarus

    3. Consider who is in your company? In what ways do these people influence your spiritual walk?

- What are the benefits of possessing fortitude in God

    1. Examine the relationship between Samson and Philistines

    2. Why should believers seek for the ability to have anchored faith?

V) Living Triumphantly!

- Acknowledging God's expectations for believers

- The ability to yield to God's will

- When you speak life, expect life to come

- Describe how the teachings within this chapter have dared you to increase your faith and expectations in God.

# THE POWER TO OVERCOME CATASTROPHE

---

"Now faith is the substance of things hoped for the evidence of things not seen."
—Hebrews 11:1 (KJV)

I) A Divine Combination

- Explain why anointing and patience is an important combination for believers to ascertain?

- What are the differences between a "come through" and a breakthrough as described within the chapter?

- What is the reward for coming through?

II) The Will to Persevere

- After reading Acts 20:1–12, describe ways in which Paul shows perseverance in ministry.

- How will you apply what you learned from the Apostle Paul's biblical example to being able to persevere in your ministry?

III) The Power of Fresh Revelation

- Why is it important for believers to remain free from distractions?

- Examine your ability to "outlast the blast."

IV) The Power to Overcome

- 🕐 Utilizing the information obtained from this chapter, define the term catastrophe

- 🕐 Reflect on the steps to overcome catastrophe.

    1. Review the testimonies or biblical examples of the men and women of God.

    2. Get anchored in Christ.

    3. Make a stance in faith.

    4. Speak out in faith.

    5. Refuse to be swayed by your flesh.

        - 🕐 Don't panic. Elevate your faith.

# THE NEXT BEST THING

> "And he said, 'I beseech thee, show me thy glory… And it shall come to pass, while my glory passeth by, that I will put thee in a clift of the rock, and will cover thee with my hand while I pass by: And I will take away mine hand, and thou shalt see my back parts: but my face shall not be seen.'"
> —Exodus 33:18, 22–23 (KJV)

I) The Worthiness and Excellency of Leadership

- 🕐 Reflect on the attributes that define excellence in leadership and that make leaders worthy of their position within an organization.

- 🕐 Examine the importance of leaders having a clear understanding of whose people they are leading.

- 🕐 Discuss five ways in which membership should show support for their leadership.

- 🕐 Examine the significance of at least one of the following statements:

    1. People will infer trustworthiness by what they perceive the level of acceptance is of that individual by their leadership.

    2. Where are you going? In the midst of it all, you are not excused to quit.

- Reflect on ways in which members can pray and intercede on behalf of their organizations for deeper relationships with God and to uphold the arms of their leadership.

II) Asking for More: Recognizing the Need for a Deeper Relationship

- Expound upon the idea "When a relationship with God is what is required for to achieve your purpose in him, you must take your gift of God that is in you and lean it in up in a corner somewhere.

- Why is it important for leaders to cultivate their faith?

- Discuss the techniques mentioned that help in building a deeper relationship with God.

III) No Face, but All Glory

- Explore the correlation between the revelation of worship and God's glory.

- Why is God's glory the next best thing?

- Reflect on experiences where you have seen God's glory.

# BLESSED, ANOINTED, AND HIGHLY FAVORED

---

*"Death and life are in the power of the tongue: and they that love it shall eat the fruit thereof."*
—Proverbs 18:21 (KJV)

I) Salutations and Greetings

- Why are salutations and greetings important?

- In what ways are salutations and greetings related to faith?

II) The Power of the Tongue

- Discuss the significance of the ability of believers to speak life over themselves and over the lives of others.

- How can believers overcome times when they may find it difficult to speak life?

- What the relationship between the heart and tongue as expounded upon in the Word of God?

III) The Principles of God's Word

- When are believers most effective when trying to get a move of God to birth deliverance? When are they least effective?

- How significant is a believer's ability to focus faith when trying to apply the principles of God to his or her life?

- 🕐 Choose at least four "power scriptures" containing salutations and benedictions as discussed in this chapter. Discuss the purpose behind choosing those scriptures and how you know they will benefit you.

IV) Blessed, Anointed, and Highly Favored

- 🕐 Reflect upon the teachings of this chapter to identify at least three personal experiences that have caused you to know that you are blessed, anointed, and highly favored.

- 🕐 Discuss at least two of the following statements:

    1. The hand of God is on your life, and the times of your life are in his hands.

    2. It took the plotting of the enemy to get you where God intended for you to be.

    3. Favor says that no matter where you find yourself, at some point, you're going to rise to the top.

# FIGHT THE DEVIL ON HIS OWN TERMS

> "For the weapons of our warfare are not carnal, but mighty through God to the pulling down of string holds; Casting down imaginations, and every high thing that exalteth itself against the knowledge of God, and bringing into captivity every thought to the obedience of Christ."
> —2 Corinthians 2:4–5 (KJV)

I) Did you know that we have weapons?

- Walking in the spirit vs. walking in the flesh

- Explain what is meant by the following statement: "You cannot win trying to war in the flesh."

- Identify and analyze the weapons afforded to us in the spirit.

II) Do you know how to *use* your spiritual weapons?

- The author makes a profound observation concerning the importance of wisdom and understanding as it relates to the use of spiritual weapons. Examine the following statement: "We are oftentimes armed with the wisdom of the canon in the spirit and lack the understanding of the .22 pistol.

- Using the knowledge obtained from the teachings in this chapter, list at least three ways in which you will utilize your spiritual gifts.

- Explain what happens as a result of believers who fail to utilize their spiritual weapons.

## III) Take It Back

- Discuss the believer's ability to spiritually "fight back in the manner that you are being fought."

- Examine the references made regarding a "par to due season" of stolen blessings?

- The significance of exercising trust and faith in God regardless of your natural perception

- The significance of praising in advance

## IV) Experiencing Victory

- Identify at least four principles that believers must be dedicated to in efforts to experience victory through the utilization of their spiritual weapons.

- How can believers fight the enemy on his own terms?

- Developing a fighter's mentality

- The power and fasting

- The significance of exercising trust and faith in God regardless of your natural perception

- The significance of praising in advance

# HOPE

> "Who against hope believed in hope, that he might become the father of many nations; according to that which was spoken so shall thy seed be."
> —Romans 4:18 (KJV)

I) Faith is the prelude to hope

- Explain why is it important to have faith?

- Discuss the phrase, "Hope is the bucket, and faith is the funnel from which it flows."

- Examine the significance of trust as it pertains to faith and hope.

II) Becoming a student of hope

- Understanding the fallibility of the flesh

- Explore the impact of the statement, "Wealth to be gained by a Christ relationship with God," and examine the ways in which we allow limitations to be placed on our relationship with God.

- Discuss one of the following prayers for the believer:

    1. "Father, please do not allow me to get in the way of what you are doing for me."

    2. "Lord, help me to please you in every way."

III) Faith sustains. Hope propels

- *Dryness vs. Solvent.* Examine the analogy of the sponge as it relates to hope and faith. How will you apply this analogy in your life?

- How instrumental is hope in fulfilling a believer's purpose?

- Can a believer's sustainability in Christ be viewed as complacency?

IV) What are you hoping for?

- Discuss ways in which we can apply the principles learned in this chapter to

    1. Hope against hope

    2. Hope beyond our current circumstances or situations

        - List at least two spiritual goals and/or natural goals that you will begin the process of hoping God for this week. Be prepared to discuss the results at the next session.

# THE IMPROBABLE MOVE OF GOD

> "Who against hope believed in hope, that he might become the father of many nations; according to that which was spoken so shall thy seed be."
> —Romans 4:18 (KJV)

I) Becoming a student of God's Deliverance

- God is everywhere concerning the believer. Personally reflect upon your experiences to identify with how God demonstrates omnipotence and omnipresence in the life of a believer.

- What is the importance in understanding God's method(s) of deliverance?

- What is the difference between God's involvement in a believer's situation as opposed to a believer forcing his or her own way of deliverance into a situation?

II) Determinations of Destiny

- Understand you have a destiny before others see it.

- Explain what is meant by the following statement: "The measure of destiny bears the weight and forms the shape that purpose will take to fulfill God's plan."

- Refuse to give up. What is prescribed does not have to be your end.

III) Agenda Driven

- Reflect on ways that you are growing the gift of God within you. Discuss ways in which you can increase growth in God.

- Acknowledging the purpose of your gift

- Why should believers prepare their gifts for the body of Christ?

IV) The Will to Fight

- Never underestimate the gift of God that is within you. Protect the gift and your influence.

- Group discussion: Are you willing to fight for the gift of God in you while it is yet in its infancy? Explain why.

- We should place greater emphasis on who we are in God, but how do we get to that place?

- Understand that your calling precedes your assignment.

- Obedience is the platform by which God will manifest himself.

# INSIDE OUT

> "But without faith it is impossible to please him: for he that cometh to God must believe that he is, and that he is a rewarder of them that diligently seek him."
>
> —Hebrews 11:6 (KJV)

I) Matters of the Heart

- Review the manner in which praise and worship should be approached.

- Identify and discuss the specific types of acts committed by a believer that will endear him or her to God?

- Reflect on the teaching within this chapter to explain why God dedicates himself to the concerns of worshippers.

II) The Road to Purpose

- Reflect on David's prayer in Psalm 13:1–6. Discuss the impact of a believer's ability to be honestly in prayer on realizing and fulfilling his or her purpose.

- Examine the significance of at least one of the following statements:

    1. It is in the crevices of what we go through that we find the evidence of where we are going to.

    2. Greatness is going in the midst of what you were called to do.

III) Don't Die Now

- Why is it important for the believer to utilize "faith to outlast your lot in life"?

- Discuss the spiritual significance of a believer's ability to speak life concerning themselves or any relevant issues concerning their lives.

- Explore the paragraph stating, "The closest God comes to hurt is his love for you." Discuss how you can use this knowledge to encourage yourself and others around you.

IV) In His Will

- Identify why it is important for believers to identify with what is in their hearts instead of approaching the things of God from an outward standpoint.

- Compare and contrast the principles of being in God's perfect will and in his permissive will.

- Explain the hidden dangers of remaining in God's permissive will.

- Remember, it is up to the believer to walk in God's perfect will for their lives.

# About The Author

Mark L. Spell began teaching and expounding on the Word of God as a pastor and founder of Disciples of Christ Deliverance Ministries (DOCDM) in June 1997. Since then, God has tremendously blessed his God-given vision of "Changing Lives through Teaching and Prayer." Pastor Spell received his bachelor's degree from North Carolina Central University and an honorary doctorate in theology from Victory International College in Durham, North Carolina.

In 2007, DOCDM expanded to become Greater Life Christian Church and has numerous outreach programs serving Raleigh, Durham, and Wilson, North Carolina.

Mark L. Spell is married to Lillian H. Spell, and they have four sons. When asked to describe her husband's work in the ministry, co-pastor Lillian Spell states, "Holiness is definitely a lifestyle for him, and his desire to see others reach their full potential is always on his heart. He is a great example that God is still moving through his people in awesome ways."

This study guide is designed to aid individuals or groups in discussing the contents of *Fresh Fire: Spiritual Transitions that Lead to Total Man Rebirth*. *Fresh Fire* was divinely inspired and written with the intentions that Christians may live to the true potential as God ordained for us. Therefore, this study guide should be approached in a practical manner in efforts to provoke believers to explore the fullness of their relationship with God.

Pastor Mark L. Spell is available for speaking engagements and ministry. For booking information, please call (919) 341-8483. You can also email your request to *admin@greaterlifechristianchurch. net* or follow Pastor Spell on Facebook at *www.facebook.com/ pastormark. spell.*

Any unauthorized reproduction or changes made to this document without the written consent of the author is strictly prohibited and subject to fines in accordance with the copyright laws that protect this document.

www.ingramcontent.com/pod-product-compliance
Lightning Source LLC
LaVergne TN
LVHW011940070526
838202LV00054B/4730